"It's good to see you, Jill. You look great."

As Vince approached, his gaze drifted over her.

"You, too." She didn't have to tell Vince he looked better than great. He probably knew it. She could imagine the babes roaming Vegas fell regularly at his feet.

He held her immobile with his dark gaze as he continued to narrow the gap between them. She could barely remember her own name, much less his. She wanted to put up her guard, but she couldn't lift a finger. And her feet...her feet weren't moving either.

He wasn't stopping. Her heart thudded against her chest.

Long arms reached for her. Settled on her shoulders and drew her to him.

Don't, don't, don't, don't…

Dear Reader,

I first met Vince in *Count on Love*. He was angry and impetuous, and caused a lot of grief to my other characters—a bad boy in need of his comeuppance! I fell in love and began devising his romantic demise. But he was a bad boy and didn't want to be tamed; not by me, not by his grandfather and certainly not by his long-lost wife, Jill.

And Jill? Jill is so used to staying the course—alone—that having an overbearing man around (much less an overbearing husband!) who interferes with every aspect of her life and makes her feel things she'd resolved never to feel again... well, it's not right. She's determined to thwart Vince at every turn, even if she and Vince were friends in school before she let him talk her into a marriage they never got around to consummating.

I hope you enjoy Jill and Vince's journey. I love to hear from readers, either via snail mail, P.O. Box 150, Denair, CA 95316, or at my Web site, www.MelindaCurtis.com, which is full of fun trivia and monthly contests.

Happy reading!

Melinda Curtis

A Marriage
Between Friends

Melinda Curtis

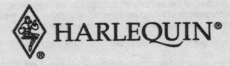

TORONTO • NEW YORK • LONDON
AMSTERDAM • PARIS • SYDNEY • HAMBURG
STOCKHOLM • ATHENS • TOKYO • MILAN • MADRID
PRAGUE • WARSAW • BUDAPEST • AUCKLAND

ISBN-13: 978-0-373-71501-5
ISBN-10:   0-373-71501-3

A MARRIAGE BETWEEN FRIENDS

www.eHarlequin.com

Printed in U.S.A.

ABOUT THE AUTHOR

Melinda Curtis lives in Northern California with her husband, three kids, two Labradors, two cats and a circle of friendly neighbors who eagerly weigh in on everything from the best way to cut your lawn to the best haircut for a fourth grader—just what good friends are for!

Books by Melinda Curtis

HARLEQUIN SUPERROMANCE

Don't miss any of our special offers. Write to us at the following address for information on our newest releases.

Harlequin Reader Service
U.S.: 3010 Walden Ave., P.O. Box 1325, Buffalo, NY 14269
Canadian: P.O. Box 609, Fort Erie, Ont. L2A 5X3

To the patient ones in my life—my dh, my cat and my editor. Good things come to those who wait!

And to the dreamers in my life—
Mason, Colby and Chelsea. It's good to dream big.

CHAPTER ONE

THE THING ABOUT RELYING only on yourself was that you had no one else to blame when things went wrong.

Vince Patrizio downshifted his Porsche 911 and hugged another hairpin turn in the California gold country. This bend in the road didn't bring Railroad Stop into view, either. *Why am I not surprised?*

His GPS didn't work in the uncharted territory at the foot of the mountains and he was unable to get a solid signal on his cell phone. He was late, lost and about to lose an important deal, one that would most likely cost him his inheritance.

Vince cursed and shifted into a higher gear, the force cocooning him deeper into the cradle of fine German leather that felt as welcoming as a well-paid stripper's back-room embrace. The car shot over a sharp rise, startling a deer next to the road. Luckily the doe ran away and down into a ravine, instead of into Vince's path.

He took a deep breath and slowed the car. It was a beautiful early-September afternoon and the narrow ribbon of road beckoned, promising he'd end up somewhere, if not exactly where he wanted to be.

The story of my life.

He'd always been a runner-up, never a winner. Born to wealth but part of a dysfunctional family, left by his wife on their wedding night, what would Vince do but screw up if faced with success and happiness?

That was his grandfather talking. Because of a card game, his grandfather had agreed to stake Vince, but only if he could put a deal together in a year. Aldo Patrizio expected Vince to fail. And for ten months Vince had been doing just that.

Vince cursed again. He jammed his foot down on the accelerator and attacked another turn.

Red lights flashed in his rearview mirror. A siren screamed.

"Now that's par for the course," Vince mumbled as he coasted into one more curve before pulling over onto the narrow shoulder beneath an ancient oak tree, hoping the sheriff was as good at giving directions as he was at speeding tickets.

"THIS MEETING IS ADJOURNED." Jill Tatum Patrizio had never been so happy to raise her gavel. Railroad Stop was safe.

"No!" Arnie Eagle grabbed the mayor's symbol of power mid-stroke, his tan fingers brushing hers.

Instinctively Jill let go of the gavel, relinquishing it to her political rival.

Why did a man's touch still rattle her after all this time?

Laughter rippled through the standing-room-only crowd at the community center, bringing Jill back to the present. Her cheeks heated. She stood and stepped back from the old warped table.

The city councilman's gaze remained fixed speculatively on Jill even as he said, "We're still waiting for our guest speaker."

That was where Jill had him. Arnie couldn't say they were still waiting for the tribe's venture capitalist to show up. That would be admitting a conflict of interest with his position on the city council.

More than aware of some three hundred Railroad Stop residents and her own son watching them, Jill lifted her chin and connected with Arnie's hard gaze. She would never support a casino in this isolated town. Railroad Stop was the kind of place where everyone knew everyone else and it was impossible not to feel at ease.

"I'm sorry, Arnie," she said. "We've rearranged the city council's agenda for you twice already. This town needs us to act to revive our economy. Since the Amador Tribal Council still lacks financing for its casino, the gated-vacation-home project will most likely garner our support. This meeting is over."

Voices filled the air. People rose to their feet. Arnie's Native American cronies began to circle him, but Jill could still feel his eyes on her. Other attendees stood and chatted or ambled out to clog the aisles. It seemed everyone but Jill was reluctant to leave, an indicator that Jill's phone would ring off the hook with calls from citizens both for and against the casino come Monday morning.

Eager to make an exit, Jill managed to reach Teddy, her ten-year-old son, and Edda Mae, her former boss and mentor. They inched their way through the throng. Edda Mae tapped a woman's shoulder with a sun-mottled, wrinkled hand and asked if they could squeeze past her. They were halfway up the side aisle and still had the rear of the room to cross.

"I would've liked to hear what Arnie's man had to say," Edna Mae said.

"Not me," Teddy piped up. "Grown-up speeches are boring, especially Mom's integer speech."

"That's integrity," Jill corrected, edging around a particularly large gentleman engrossed in a heated discussion about the merits of a casino versus a vacation subdivision. "Don't knock it. That's what got me elected."

"You were the only one who ran," Edda Mae said.

"That doesn't mean no one else cares," Jill grumbled, bumped from behind by someone.

There was a commotion at the exit doors.

"Either Arnie's man finally arrived," Edda Mae said, "or the Staitin brothers picked a fight again."

Jill wasn't sure which was worse.

ALDO PATRIZIO wasn't listening. The conference room at the Sicilian in Las Vegas was full of pompous men in designer suits who thought their college degrees made them more qualified to run a luxury casino than the man in his eighties who'd founded it in the first place. At least when his grandson, Vince, sat at this table, there had been some interesting ideas and a man with backbone to present them.

Che peccato. It was a shame that after Vince returned from Iraq they'd shouted themselves into a corner neither was willing to back out of.

Aldo snorted and the suit currently babbling in front of a projection screen froze in midsentence. When the man resumed, he spoke louder, as if Aldo had trouble hearing him. Aldo could hear just fine. He just didn't want to listen to people who'd barely cut their teeth in the gambling business try to tell him what to do. What he did want was to pass the reins of the Sicilian to his grandson and spend more time with his beloved Rosalie.

Instead, Vince was off trying to prove himself by brokering a deal—a deal that had seemed important to both of them ten months ago—while Aldo had to sit and suffer through meetings with MBAs (Masters of Baloney, Advanced).

"In conclusion—"

Good, they were almost done.

"Our analysis has shown that independent casinos fail over time if not infused with a good deal of capital."

Aldo narrowed his eyes at the audacity of the speaker, who cleared his throat and continued, "Therefore, we recommend that the Sicilian formulate exit strategies from current partnerships, such as the ones with the Tatums, that we cease efforts to enter the Native American gaming segment, and that we seriously reconsider recent buyout offers from two different casino magnates."

"Enough!" Aldo slapped his palm on the mahogany table and glared at his chief financial officer. "What is our occupancy rate?"

The man rotated his chin as if his tie was too tight. "Over ninety-eight percent."

"How do our room rates compare to others along The Strip?"

"We charge five percent more on average."

"And our restaurants. Do we still have five-star ratings at all of them?"

Heads bobbed silently around the room. A bigger collection of *jamooks* he'd never seen.

"And our casino profits, are they also above average?"

More nodding heads.

"Then why would I want to sell?" Aldo slapped the table again for good measure.

When no one answered, Aldo stood, willing his old knees to hold up as he nailed each traitor with his glare. "I pay you to bring my vision to life, not to create a new one."

Next thing you knew they'd be declaring him incompetent and trying to take over the control of his casino!

"IT'S HIM."

"He's here."

Vince stood in the open doorway only a moment before arms pulled him into the packed community center like fans welcoming a rock star.

This is good. This is better than good.

"Let him through," a man bellowed from the front of the large, ancient hall.

"The town council meeting is over," said someone from the far side of the room. It was impossible to see who it was in the sea of faces or, over the noise, make out more than that the speaker was a woman.

"Then we'll call a meeting of the Amador Tribal Council. I hereby call this meeting to order." A man with distinguished gray in the dark hair at his temples took up a position behind the front table. With the strong features and bronze skin, he had to be the tribal chairman, Arnie Eagle. Vince had spoken with him several times about providing the bulk of the financing for a casino.

Chairs scraped and banged as people fought for a seat. A few men hurried to fill the spots at the table while others moved to stand behind them.

Pausing only to tug his starched cuffs farther down his wrists, Vince pasted on his warmest smile and walked to the podium.

"Good evening. I apologize for being late. My name is Vince Patrizio."

Someone in the crowd made a strangled noise. Chairs creaked and he heard his last name muttered throughout the room.

A nugget of his prior conversation with Arnie returned.

"Are you related to—"

"Yes." Vince hurriedly cut off the chairman's question during their initial phone call, assuming that Arnie wanted to know if he was related to Aldo Patrizio, the self-made tycoon.

Vince needed to find out if his grandfather's name was an advantage or a deal breaker. Meanwhile, his smile never faltered. "I may have been invited here at the request of the tribal council, but I hope that when I'm through most of you will see the benefits of a casino in Railroad Stop. Indulge me for a moment as I recap the advantages of having such a facility in your area."

Off to his right, someone scoffed, someone Vince would have to deal with soon, just not in front of such a large audience.

Vince spoke briefly of job opportunities, the tax dollars that would go to improving roads and schools, as well as the fact that Railroad Stop could control how big the casino would be. Vince hoped for big. "Raising a family, paying the bills and building a community all take hard work and vision. I encourage you to talk amongst yourselves, to foster healthy debates like this one."

"You haven't invited us to debate you. Big companies don't usually care about small facilities." A woman's voice. From the right wall. Heckler Central.

There were several murmurs of assent.

Who *was* this woman? Vince couldn't tell. And he wouldn't validate her remarks by acknowledging them. It didn't matter. The time for discussion would come later, after he'd created a platform of enthusiasm and support.

Vince continued as if uninterrupted. "If you feel a casino built to represent the character and heritage of the area will help bring to life the vision you have for Railroad Stop's future, I'll be happy to help you achieve that."

His comments were met with a healthy dose of applause, but Vince wasn't fooled. Deliberately, he turned to his right, preparing a friendly smile for the vocal naysayer he needed to win over. As if on cue, all the others in the crowd angled their heads toward one woman as well, unwittingly pointing her out.

Despite the mutinous expression on her face, she avoided his gaze. She wore flannel and blue jeans like most of the crowd, but that didn't hide her polish. She wore the casual clothes with style.

A vein throbbed in Vince's forehead. It wasn't his grandfather the murmuring crowd had been thinking about.

The tremble of Jill's auburn ponytail gave away that his *wife* wasn't happy to see him.

The feeling was mutual.

"HE'S GOT OUR last name." Teddy bobbed and weaved in front of Jill as he tried to catch a glimpse of Vince. "Why is that?"

It could have been Jill's imagination that everyone within five feet of her stopped talking and leaned closer, anxiously awaiting her answer, but it wasn't, which was why she chose to ignore her son's question. Several townspeople were already streaming down the aisle with eyes on Jill. And those that weren't had Vince in their sights. The crush of inquisitive people forced Jill, Teddy and Edda Mae back down to the front of the hall, toward her husband. It was easy to pretend in the chaos that she couldn't hear anyone's questions directed her way.

"Is he your man?" Edda Mae asked, the tanned skin around her eyes wrinkled, more than usual with the width of her hopeful smile. "I bet he's come to claim you."

"If he wanted to, Vince would have come after me years ago." Jill's limbs trembled.

In the eleven years they'd been married Vince had become a shadow of her own making, always with her but never truly there. Silent and malleable, her image of Vince had been perfect for Jill. Until the real man showed up supporting the wrong cause.

And flashing his pearly whites at Arnie.

"Time to go, Teddy." Jill nudged his shoulder.

The crowd at the front of the hall parted to let them through. And why wouldn't they? Jill was providing enough fodder for a year's worth of gossip. And now she had to pass within arm's reach of Vince to leave.

"Are you going to ask him why we have the same last name?" Teddy spun about and grabbed her arm, tilting his head up so that Jill could see the impish grin on his face.

"No."

"Can I?"

"No." Jill gently turned her son around and continued working her way toward the exit. The last time she'd seen her husband he'd been asleep on the couch in the house her parents had given them as a wedding gift and she'd been tiptoeing out the door. He'd never asked for an explanation for her departure and she'd never offered one.

Jill was now close enough to take in Vince's crisp haircut, the fine thread count of his jacket as it stretched across his broad shoulders, and the smile that had melted more than one girl's heart. At least his leather shoes had a layer of dust on them. Otherwise he'd have been fashionably spotless, whereas she looked dowdy in her worn jeans and shirt.

Vince was listening intently to the council chairman, Arnie Eagle. He wouldn't even notice her leaving. It was probably her imagination that he'd recognized her at all.

As Jill drew even with Vince's shoulder, she couldn't resist saying half under her breath, "I won't let you build a casino here."

Vince held up a hand, stopping Arnie midsentence—no small feat—and turned to Jill, his dark gaze commanding. "We'll discuss that—and more—later."

Teddy's eyes were as big as saucers.

"Ohhh," Edda Mae sighed as if this was a scene in one of her beloved romance novels.

Without a word, Jill made her escape. It wasn't until her hand hesitated with the key in the ignition that she realized she'd nodded her assent.

"YOU'VE BEEN very patient." With the rolling gait of a veteran horseman, Arnie escorted Vince out, his flashlight illuminating the dirt road.

"Everyone deserves their questions answered," Vince said. Arnie didn't realize that nothing was ruining this one for Vince, not potholed roads or longlost wives who tossed down the gauntlet without so much as a *how've you been.*

"But you're probably anxious to see your family," Arnie said, unable to hide his curiosity.

Vince bit back a bitter laugh. Jill wasn't family. He knew she'd settled in Railroad Stop. But he hadn't expected her to treat him as if he'd been the one who left.

"I've got four of our tribal-council members behind this project. Our vote is just a formality if your offer is fair." Arnie's voice dragged Vince's attention back.

He smiled. Vince was willing to take a chance on Arnie. A graduate of Stanford, Arnie had made a respectable fortune selling his interest in a dot.com before the industry busted. Even if the casino venture wasn't a sure thing, Arnie and his colleagues had conducted an environmental-impact study last year and hired an architect to draw up plans. They were further down the path than any other tribe Vince had contacted recently, and his best bet.

"Then comes the challenge," Arnie said. "Getting Railroad Stop to agree. We'll have one more town meeting and then the city council makes a recommendation and the citizens vote. If it weren't for our mayor, I'd say we'd have a really good chance."

At least now Vince knew what, or rather, who, was priority number one. "Leave the mayor to me."

Arnie chuckled. "I plan to."

Before Vince had a chance to ask Arnie more about the mayor they reached his car.

"Is this fancy rig yours?" Arnie stopped and bathed Vince's black Porsche in the beam of his flashlight. "You'll need four-wheel drive come November."

"Not very practical for up here, is it?" Vince allowed, not that he planned to drive anything else but the sleek bullet. Venture capitalists had to look successful. Appearances were everything. "Can you give me directions to the nearest hotel?" It was best to get that business over with early so he could focus on the mayor. He would check in and then head over to Jill's.

"There are no hotels in Railroad Stop. You could drive about forty-five minutes down the mountain to Mokelumne Hill, but there's a storm brewing and it's going to get nasty." Arnie paused, watching Vince carefully as he said, "You should probably just head on over to Shady Oak. Jill bought the place from Edda Mae last spring. She's got enough beds to spare, I'm guessing."

Vince's thumb paused on the car remote. "I thought you said there were no hotels in town."

"Jill doesn't run a hotel. She turned the Shady Oak from a kids' camp into a fancy corporate retreat.

Thought you'd know that, seeing as how you two are married." Arnie's gaze was speculative in the gloom.

What else didn't Vince know about his wife? Maybe it was time to update her background check.

When Vince remained silent, Arnie cleared his throat. "You want me to tell you how to get to Shady Oak? That land we put into federal trust for the casino is in the valley below her place."

Vince almost refused the offer of directions. And then he remembered that Railroad Stop didn't register on his GPS.

CHAPTER TWO

"HOW'S THIS?" Teddy asked, rocking back on his heels to survey his work, a paintbrush in each hand. He had an artistic bent and instead of choosing a plain color for the background of the signs Jill planned to post against the casino, her son had created psychedelic bursts with the purple and green paint left over from the last time they'd decorated his room.

"Brilliant," Jill said. "Just a few more and we'll call it a night."

They worked on the uphill side of Shady Oak's garage underneath a floodlight. Jill had been cutting plywood into two-foot-by-three-foot pieces with a cordless skill saw while Teddy worked his magic. The eye-catching swirls of color would contrast perfectly with the important message Jill planned to spray-paint with stenciled block letters in red—NO CASINO!

She returned her saw to its case and then propped up the last two boards against the garage wall, taking another look at Teddy's artwork, while her mind wandered. She, the daughter of casino owners, was opposing a casino. Jill could picture the worried look in her mother's eyes, her father's disapproving frown, and Vince's face…

For years she'd recalled Vince's youthful features fondly, but those images had been shattered tonight by a strong jaw, a suit he hadn't bought off the rack, and his corporate stance. Once she'd recovered from the shock of his arrival, it had been easy to see through his words, to see that he'd become one of *them*—someone like her parents and his grandfather. Vince planned to milk the heart out of Railroad Stop, turning it into a miniature Vegas.

When Jill left Las Vegas eleven years ago, she'd wanted to find a place where she could feel safe, where she could take people at their word. On a sweltering Saturday, less than a week later, she'd gotten a flat tire in Railroad Stop. Edda Mae had taken one look at Jill, wilting while she waited for her car, and herded her into Bernie's Burger Joint. In no time the older woman had pried the pertinent facts out of Jill, told her a story about one of her Native American ancestors and convinced Jill that running away never solved anything. Jill had gone to work for Edda Mae at Shady Oak the next day.

Edda Mae was the mother figure Jill had always longed for, and for the most part, Railroad Stop embraced Jill. After Teddy was born she stayed on, unable to curb her overactive imagination when it came to Shady Oak. Jill was still her parents' daughter and the hospitality industry was in her blood. Where others might have seen a hopeless money pit, Jill had envisioned charming success. When Edda Mae was ready to retire, Jill took out an exorbitantly scary loan cosigned by her parents and employee became employer.

"So." Teddy crouched over one of the last two boards and began creating a curvy purple road. He was a gangly kid, all knobby elbows and knees, an aficionado of bad jokes, but he was her pride and joy. "Who is he?"

"Who?" Jill tried to play dumb.

"The man from the meeting. Is he your cousin?"

"No."

"Your brother?"

"No." Jill half carried, half dragged one of the old wooden sawhorses back into the storage shed.

Teddy was into the lime-green paint when she returned, tracing a curvy line with the color. "Why does he have our last name?"

"All right, all right. I'll tell you." Wiping her hands on the seat of her jeans, Jill drew a dramatic breath. "He's Batman and he's taken on an alias so that he can continue fighting injustice to protect the innocent." Although Jill didn't let Teddy watch much television, she'd broken down and joined a mail-order video-rental service a few weekends before, introducing Teddy to the crime fighter.

"Mo-om." Teddy stopped painting. He had a way of looking at Jill that said, *Cut the BS*. "I'm ten, not two."

"It's complicated." Jill poked the ground with one toe. They'd talked about Jill's separate-but-married status, but lately Teddy had wanted to know more about his father, the man he assumed Jill had married. She didn't want to tell Teddy he was a rape-conceived child—he was too young to carry that baggage—so she'd resorted to jokes and topic changes.

Something stirred delicately near a leaf by Jill's foot—a spider. "Eeeeeiiii!!" She leaped a yard away, stumbling backward up the slope. Just the thought of eight spindly legs creeping across her skin gave her the willies.

Teddy dutifully came over with a rolled-up newspaper. "It's just a baby." He scooped it up and took it behind the shed.

"Baby?" It was the size of a fifty-cent piece. "I wish you'd kill it."

"Spiders are good bugs, remember?" Teddy's voice was muffled. He galloped back waving the newspaper. "All gone."

Jill shivered. "He'll be back."

Edda Mae appeared at the corner of the garage. "I buzzed that casino man in the front gate."

That was what Jill got for trying to cut costs. The main gate was a quarter mile down the hill. Its intercom rang to Edda Mae's caretaker's cottage. It had been significantly cheaper to wire the gate controls to the cottage since it was a hundred feet closer than the apartment above the dining hall/kitchen where Jill and Teddy lived.

"Need I remind you to watch your manners?" Edda Mae asked as she melted back into the shadows. Edda Mae probably expected Jill to race down the road into Vince's arms.

"I wouldn't have had to mind my manners if the gate stayed locked," Jill muttered.

Gravel crunched beneath tires on the driveway and headlights swung around onto them and then away as Vince parked out of sight in front of the garage. A smooth engine roared once before settling into silence.

He'd want a divorce. Jill spun her wedding ring with her left thumb. It wasn't as if she was going to ask for alimony or child support from Vince. A divorce shouldn't be a big deal, although odd as it seemed, being married to Vince was part of who she was. But if she had to choose, preserving the small-town integrity of Railroad Stop was more important than a ring on her finger.

"Jill?" Vince's voice was deep and familiar when so much about her husband was a mystery.

A breath of cool mountain air made Jill shiver. "Over here."

They'd gone to private school together since kindergarten. In high school, Vince was the class loner, a situation he and his perpetual scowl seemed comfortable with, especially when it didn't seem to deter a certain type of willing girl. Jill was the brainy girl who didn't quite fit in. Although they'd been friends of sorts since they were five, the older they got, the less frequently their paths crossed.

Then Vince had asked Jill to come watch the sunset on his boat on Senior Ditch Day. But Craig had been coming over to her house that evening and Craig was so perfect—captain of every sports team, class president—no girl would be stupid enough to turn him down. Whereas Vince...Vince was the kind of boy her parents warned her about.

Jill struggled to fill her lungs with air. Turned out Craig wasn't so perfect, after all, and Vince...

Teddy balanced his paintbrush on the edge of the can and leaned against Jill, bringing her back to the present. "Is it Batman?" he whispered.

They both giggled. Jill draped an arm over Teddy's shoulders as Vince came around the corner in his custom-made suit and tie, looking every inch the heir to a grand casino in Las Vegas and draining the laughter from her throat. The rebellious boy who wore a leather jacket and pierced his ear was nowhere to be seen in this man. Jill, on the other hand, had gone from put-together, studious debutante to harried, working single mom. Her stomach flip-flopped.

"It's good to see you, Jill. You look great." As Vince approached, his gaze drifted over her, no doubt registering the extra pounds she'd put on over the years.

"You, too." She didn't have to tell Vince he looked better than great. He probably knew it. Jill could imagine the plastic babes roaming Vegas falling regularly at his feet. If only she could easily picture Vince turning them down. He must think she was a pathetic pushover for hanging on to him for so long.

Vince held Jill immobile with his dark gaze as he continued to narrow the gap between them. Hugging had become de rigueur in the business world in the past ten years. Surely he didn't...

Part of her rejoiced. That unexpected emotion was immediately quelled by a stronger, more predictable desire for self-preservation that usually gave Jill the strength to move away, raise a hand and smoothly utter an excuse for a man to keep his distance.

Only, this time she faltered. She could barely remember her own name, much less his. She wanted to put up her guard, but couldn't lift a finger. And her feet...her feet weren't moving, either.

He wasn't stopping. Jill's heart thudded against her chest.

By sheer force of will she managed to take a jerky step back. Surely he'd see her discomfort. He'd always been good at picking up on her body language, but it had been so long he probably didn't realize. Long arms reached for her. Large hands settled on her shoulders and drew her to him.

Don't, don't, don't, don't... "Don't!" she cried, her feet suddenly obeying her mind. Her butt hit the remaining sawhorse and she would have flipped over it, but Vince held her tight.

"I'M NOT GOING to support your casino." Wary-eyed, Jill wrenched herself free from his grip and edged around the sawhorse until it stood between them.

"Mom? Are you okay?"

"I'm...fine." She gave her son a weak smile.

"Jill?" That unwanted protective male instinct, the one only Jill aroused, had reawakened. Vince wiped his palms, still warm from touching her, against his trousers and stepped away.

"I'm fine," Jill repeated, hefting one end of the sawhorse and dragging it toward the open shed behind the garage. "I'm not supporting your casino."

"I haven't asked you to," Vince snapped, taking the other end of the sawhorse and examining her face, hoping to find a reason for his old obsession.

Jill stumbled under his scrutiny, but kept walking backward.

On the first day of kindergarten Jill had stuck up for Vince in front of a teacher, and he'd contracted a bad case of puppy love that continued through childhood only to fizzle out less than a year after their wedding day. She was pretty enough, but no longer his type. He liked his women pouty and aggressive in bed, women who didn't mind that he wore a wedding ring and wasn't interested in anything long-term. Vince took note of how high up Jill had buttoned her flannel shirt.

Nope. He was definitely over her.

"Just so you know," Jill said woodenly, "people come here to get away from it all. Having a casino at the turnoff to Shady Oak doesn't exactly reinforce that feeling of peaceful solitude."

Vince didn't want to talk about the casino. "The two can coexist."

"Not on my mountain." Taking baby steps, Jill led him into the gloomy, crowded shed. Once the sawhorse was on the floor and the only barrier between Jill and the door was Vince, she froze, watching her husband from the shadows as if scared of him.

Of *him.* As if he'd been the one who attacked her. Could the day get any worse? Vince stubbornly refused to move, waiting for Jill to show some backbone. "I don't think you own the entire mountain."

"No." She still didn't move.

They stared at each other in silence for several seconds more.

With a sigh, Vince backed out of the shed and into the boy.

Craig's son.

The vivid blue eyes and reddish-brown hair were Jill's. Try as he might, Vince couldn't see anything in this kid of the solidly built, blond mama's boy who'd date-raped Jill.

"Who are you?" the kid asked.

"Vince Patrizio." Vince offered his hand and took the opportunity to lead the boy back to the garage.

The smell of new wood permeated the crisp mountain air. From what he could see, Shady Oak was a replica of an old Western town. There were small bungalows with covered plank porches and wooden rocking chairs. The garage was painted to look like a red barn. A two-story 1800s-style building with a sign across large double doors proclaimed it to be Edda Mae's Dining Emporium. The entire place would have looked like a kids' movie set, except there was no landscaping, just dirt and pine trees.

"I'm Teddy Patrizio. We have the same last name." Teddy cast a questioning sideways glance at Vince.

Vince was only half listening, still thinking about Jill's Western corporate retreat, a concept very similar to the themed casinos in Vegas. "It's a good last name. It's Italian. I'm happy to share it."

Jill hurried past, picking up a tool chest on her way to the front of the garage. Wearing boot-cut jeans, her legs looked long and Vince found it hard not to follow her every move with his eyes until he realized he had an audience.

Another sidelong stare from the boy. This one appraising. "I don't look anything like you."

"Teddy!" Jill turned at the corner of the building, her voice giving away her distress.

The kid leaned closer to Vince and whispered, "I know who you are."

Premonition prickled the hair on the back of Vince's neck and he found himself bending lower.

"Theodore Tatum Patrizio!" Jill's gaze collided with Vince's, a plea for help in her eyes, but Vince didn't understand what she needed.

And it was suddenly important that Vince knew who her son thought he was.

"You're Batman." Teddy smirked at Vince, then winked at his mother. "Right, Mom?"

"Teddy." Jill shook her head, looking incredibly relieved. "That wasn't funny."

"You've lost me," Vince said.

"It was a joke." All traces of humor gone, Teddy knelt and picked up a paintbrush as his mother disappeared into the garage. "You're not my dad," the boy said in a dejected voice after a few brush strokes.

Vince hadn't expected such honesty from one so young. "No, I'm not."

"But you're related to me."

Watching them, Jill hesitated at the corner of the garage.

"Well, I married—"

"Vince, no!"

"—your mother."

"You *are* my dad. I knew it." Teddy jumped up, tossed the paintbrush on a scrap of newspaper and flung his arms around Vince.

His palm landed awkwardly on top of Teddy's soft auburn hair.

"Teddy. Teddy, let go, baby." Jill was at Vince's feet, pulling Teddy back to her. But the boy only clung tighter to Vince. "Teddy, he's not your father." Jill skewered Vince with a look.

"But you're married." The boy stared at his mother with eyes suddenly welling with tears.

Jill shook her head and drew Teddy away from Vince.

"But—"

"Your father didn't want…" Jill's voice trailed off and she looked at Vince helplessly.

Teddy cut a quick glance in Vince's direction. "You didn't want me?"

"Dad, I'll be good. I promise. Don't leave." Trying not to cry, Vince blocked the door. But his father was bigger and stronger and had no trouble easing Vince aside. Had no trouble leaving without looking back.

"I always wanted you." On impulse Vince put a hand on Teddy's skinny shoulder. He'd been ready to take on the responsibility of fatherhood and give this boy the love he deserved. When he'd asked Jill to marry him he'd told her that everyone deserved to be loved, even a baby you hadn't counted on.

"Vince, don't build his hopes," Jill warned.

Teddy wiped tears from his cheeks and gazed up at Vince reverently. In that moment, Vince would have done anything for the kid.

"You always think things are more complicated than they are," Vince said softly, unable to take his eyes off Teddy.

"And you always believe you've found the best and only solution."

Vince scowled and stared pointedly at his ring on her left hand. "You married me, didn't you?" He hadn't noticed the ring before and wondered why it was still there. There was no way she wore it for the same reason he did.

"So…are you my dad?" Teddy broke in, his bottom lip trembling as he looked from Jill to Vince.

The truth would take some of the shine out of the

kid's eyes and Vince was reluctant to do it. But the truth had to be said. "No."

Jill spread her arms and Teddy filled them. Vince's urge to drop to his knees and be a part of that embrace was surprisingly strong.

"Your father wasn't ready to be a dad, Teddy. But from the moment I saw you, Teddy, I loved you." Jill's expression was fierce, kindling an ache in Vince's chest. No one had ever claimed to feel that way about him. "I wanted you, Teddy. I was willing to do anything to protect you, even marry someone else, someone other than your dad, and move up here."

Vince had been reduced to nothing more than a "someone else" in her life, not even a friend. If that wasn't his cue to leave Vince didn't know what was. But first he had to find out why Jill was against the casino. He needed as much support as he could get.

"But he's here now." His voice high-pitched and desperate, Teddy pointed at Vince. "He's here and he could be my dad."

Dad. This boy thought he was father material. Vince wouldn't know how or where to begin to be a father. His own had given up on him after fourteen years. Still…

"He can't be your dad," Jill was saying.

"Wait a minute," Vince said, causing Teddy to beam, which in turn made Vince's heart swell—this little boy wanted him for a dad!

"A father is there for you every day, in every way. Vince lives in Las Vegas."

"Oh." Vince and Teddy were simultaneously brought crashing back to earth. Vince realized his toes were cold. Who was he kidding? No way was he father material.

Teddy wiped his face with his hands and then stood dejectedly, shifting on his long, skinny feet.

Jill kissed Teddy's cheek. "I think we've done enough painting for one night. Why don't you go on upstairs and get yourself some ice cream?"

"Three scoops?" Teddy sniffed, sneaking a glance at Vince.

"Two." Jill wrapped her arms around the kid, only releasing him when he squirmed free. "I'll be up soon to tuck you in."

Teddy shuffled across the gravel driveway to a covered staircase. Vince's anger grew with each step Teddy took as he climbed to the second story, but he held it in check until a door clicked closed.

"It's been more than ten years, Jill. You haven't told him anything about me."

Jill jerked her head as if in shock, sending her auburn ponytail cascading over one shoulder. "You're not his father, Vince."

"But I *am* your husband." Not that he knew what that meant. Vince rubbed his forehead. He hadn't come here to reclaim his wife. Vince should just slide back into the leather seat of his Porsche and instruct his attorney to draw up the divorce papers. He reached in his pocket for his car keys, but couldn't seem to pull them out. "I told you when I asked you to marry me that I'd love your baby as if he were my own."

"I know." Jill looked away and lowered her voice. "Teddy's been without a father for ten years because of me. I had some hard choices to make, but I'm willing to live with them." And then she did look at him, squaring her shoulders. "Besides, you only came now because a business deal made it convenient. I don't expect you to step into the fatherhood role after all this time."

"Then what do you expect?" But Vince knew. Money. He flexed his fingers. It always came down to money, and Arnie had mentioned her buying this place. Shady Oak couldn't have been cheap. "We're still married. My family made a deal with yours. It's been quite profitable." Vince glared at Jill. They hadn't signed a prenuptial agreement.

"How dare you imply—"

"How dare you *leave* me!" Vince lost the struggle with his temper. "You got what you wanted—a name to legitimize Teddy—and I've let you keep it all these years, no questions asked. Well, now you can damn well answer a few of them."

CHAPTER THREE

"PLEASE DON'T YELL." Jill felt Vince's anger pulse over her. She hadn't realized how much she'd hurt him back then.

And yet she couldn't tell him the real reason she'd left, because Vince was nothing like the memory of the man she'd carried with her all these years. He wasn't patient. He wasn't kind. He didn't...

He'd never understand, and she'd had enough dreams shattered for one day.

Ignoring the way the cool air had her shivering, Jill turned her back on Vince and picked up Teddy's paintbrush. There were two more boards to paint.

"I'm sorry," Vince said after several seconds sounding anything but. He sighed.

Jill tried to ignore him. First thing tomorrow she'd spray-paint two powerful words on all of the signs. By the afternoon she'd have them up all over town and then she could make the guest beds, hang the linens and stock the rooms with toiletries in preparation for a new group of clients checking in Sunday afternoon.

And Vince—both the real and her fantasy version— would most likely be gone.

A pang of loneliness settled in her bones.

Of course, it could have been the cold. It was quite nippy now.

Vince's Italian loafers moved closer as Jill splashed a curve of purple jerkily across the board. But Vince said nothing, and then his feet disappeared. A car door opened and closed.

Jill's shoulders sagged. The Vince she'd fashioned over the years wouldn't have let the conversation end, wouldn't have left. He'd have stayed and faced the situation head-on.

"What kind of crazy stuff are they assigning school-kids nowadays?" Vince crouched next to Jill and picked up the other paintbrush. He'd taken off his expensive jacket and tucked his tie in the placket of his shirt.

"It's...um...crazy." Jill repressed the urge to smile. If the man didn't have enough sense to leave she wasn't going to tell him he was helping the opposition. Smooth and graceful, his line of green more closely resembled Teddy's style than hers. It was only guilt that made her admit, "You're good with a brush."

Vince flashed her the smile he'd given the tribal council.

"But this isn't rocket science, so I'm not impressed." Jill went back to her own stiff lines as the wind rustled through the branches above them. The storm that was supposed to pass through during the night was building. The road to Mokelumne was tricky enough in daylight. Add darkness and rain and it was dangerous. "You're not Monet. You can paint faster."

"I don't think Teddy would appreciate something just thrown together."

"You'd be surprised."

A faint roll of thunder sounded in the distance. The boards were on the east side of the garage sheltered by an overhang. They'd be protected tonight. If Vince didn't leave soon, Jill wouldn't be.

"Switch brushes." Jill dipped her brush in purple and handed the dripping mess to him.

Vince was more meticulous in his pass-off. The green didn't so much as dribble off the brush when he gave it to her, reminding Jill how graceful he was. She'd always struggled to be the polished sophisticate, while he could carry off class in worn jeans and a T-shirt. He was probably an accomplished lover, too.

"You're smearing the paint," Vince pointed out. "You've got a big black blotch where the green and purple mix. Why don't you turn that one over and start again?"

It was on the tip of Jill's tongue to tell Vince the blotches didn't matter. By tomorrow there'd be something covering up her sloppy work. "This will do."

"Here. I'll fix it." Vince edged closer, reaching his arms in front of her so that he could pick up her board. Long arms, long fingers, long—

"It's fine." That self-preservation kicked in again. No longer cold, Jill elbowed Vince back into his own space, sending a glob of green paint flying onto one of his fine Italian-leather shoes. She snatched up a scrap of newspaper and tried to wipe the goop off, but the paint had already soaked into the leather, leaving a dime-size mark.

"I'm sorry. I'm always such a klutz."

"Some things never change." Vince laughed, a rich sound that seeped into Jill's system and made her want to relax until she looked in his dark eyes and saw the same lure of heat that had made her heart pound when she was a teenager. Now her heart nearly stopped. Was she destined to be simultaneously intimidated and drawn to Vince?

As if sensing her confusion, Vince let his laughter fade away. His gaze trapped hers.

Thunder grumbled in the distance.

"You say that like it's a good thing." Turning away, Jill slapped paint on the last bare corners of her board. The wind had picked up, quivering the tree limbs overhead. "It's getting late. You need to go before the storm comes."

WHAT HAPPENED HERE?

One minute Vince was convinced Jill was out to fleece him and the next she had him eating out of her hand, only to send him away as if she hadn't noticed the sparks between them. Which, considering their past, shouldn't surprise him.

Vince had driven out to Shady Oak for some answers and had come up empty. Jill had ignored his demands to know why she'd left and he'd forgotten—*forgotten*—to ask her why she wasn't going to support the casino. Frustration burned beneath his skin, and the pent-up energy demanded release.

Vince fired up the Porsche, toying with the idea of gunning it down the driveway as if he were a broken-hearted teenager. Maturity won out only because the gravel would pepper his fenders. Instead, Vince backed out quickly and took off with just a bit more gas than was wise.

The sky ignited with lightning, and thunder bellowed so close it shook the car.

His headlights picked up a smoking pink housecoat.

Vince slammed on the brakes. He'd almost taken out an old woman in curlers walking her poofy, volleyball-size, white dog. And indulging in a pipe.

The thunder faded away.

Vince's heart started beating again. He turned off the engine, left the lights on and hopped out into the windy night. "Sorry about that. Are you okay?"

Silver curlers glinted in the car's beams. The old woman drew the pipe slowly from her mouth. "I nearly peed my pants. Think Moonbeam piddled herself. How 'bout you?"

Relief had him grinning. "Pretty damn close."

Moonbeam's white hair stuck out like porcupine quills, but whether that was from fright or her natural state, Vince didn't know.

"Name's Edda Mae. I buzzed you in the gate." The woman drew on her pipe, sending wisps of smoke curling into the air. "Saw you speak in town. I had hopes for you, boy."

"The project is in the early stages. Don't give up on me yet."

"Wasn't talkin' about your money." Edda Mae gestured with her pipe to the glowing windows above the Edda Mae's Dining Emporium sign.

Vince glanced up at Jill's place, allowing the woman to make assumptions. Jill had left Vegas and made something of herself while he'd flailed around without a clear purpose. A better man might not have felt jealousy. In any case, he'd get this casino off the ground despite Jill's opposition, and then he'd finally feel as if he'd accomplished something.

Fat drops fell in a faltering pattern around them.

"Shouldn't be out in this weather. You got a place to stay?" Edda Mae's gaze was piercing.

"No."

"You best park that thing over here. Don't know why young bucks need to drive like they're havin' bad sex." She turned toward a miniature house on the downhill side of the garage. "Fast, fast, fast. What a waste."

"Beg pardon?" He couldn't have heard her right.

"The rain's come," Edda Mae said, her eyes trained on the rocky ground as she walked away. "The road won't be safe. You'll have to stay here tonight. Best hurry before I change my mind, boy." As Edda Mae climbed the steps to the narrow covered front porch, the rain arrived with a roar, sending Vince scrambling for cover.

A few minutes later he sat on an antique brocade love seat with worn-out cushions and wood trim that creaked every time he breathed. The small cottage was crammed with an eclectic mix of possessions—Native American baskets and pottery, a short section of picket fence leaning against a wall, a 49ers calendar from two years ago—and smelled of tobacco. Moonbeam sat just out of reach and stared at Vince with dark, beady eyes.

"Whiskey?" Edda Mae asked, seemingly unconcerned that she was entertaining in her pink chenille robe and curlers.

"Beer?" he countered.

"Coffee?"

"Black. Let me help you." Vince leaned forward to stand, but Moonbeam started yapping. Vince sat back again.

"Moonbeam doesn't like strangers in the house. Best stay where you are. Besides, Jill gave me one of those newfangled coffee machines last Christmas."

Vince slid to the end of the couch. The little beast pranced along with him, growling. Vince scowled at her. They were still having a face-off when Edda Mae came out with two mugs.

She handed the steaming one to Vince and then parked herself in a big brown recliner. "You aren't a dog person, are you."

"Never had one." The ceramic mug was too hot to hold. Vince set it on a coaster on the antique end table.

Still growling, Moonbeam tilted sideways along with his arm. All it would take is one swift boot...

Edda Mae took a swig from her cup and studied Vince through faded brown eyes that seemed too knowing. "Everybody should have a dog. They're man's best friend."

Vince shook his head. Moonbeam's nose twitched. The dog was annoying but cute. He could never really hurt her.

"Ever own a cat?"

"No."

"Canary?"

"No."

The rain came down with hail-like ferocity. Moonbeam licked her chops as if anticipating an Italian snack.

"That's just not right." Edda Mae imbibed a bit

more and then pinned him with squinty eyes. "You ain't been around for Teddy."

Vince opened his mouth to explain that he wasn't the boy's father, but thought better of it. Moonbeam's snarl filled the air, instead.

A framed picture of Jill holding a baby with ruddy cheeks and a gummy grin caught his eye. "You watch out for Jill," Vince observed, feeling unexpectedly empty. "I should go."

If Vince slept on the antique love seat, he'd have to hang his legs over the side, and he was certain to wake up with kinks in several places.

"No need. I'll get you set for the night. Jill's an early riser."

Edda Mae stood with the exacting precision of one who doesn't always feel stable on her feet when she first gets up. "Come along."

Ignoring Moonbeam's noisy protests, Vince steadied Edda Mae, moving her toward what he took to be a closet where he guessed she kept the extra bedding.

Edda Mae dug in her heels. "I'm not going to let you into my bedroom, young man. We've only just met."

He released the old woman. "I'm sorry. If you give me a blanket, I'll make the bed." Vince tried not to look at the love seat.

Now it was Edda Mae's turn to take his arm, steering him toward the door. "You're not sleeping with me. You're sleeping with Jill."

Much as the idea appealed to Vince, he was sure Jill would think differently. "Why don't you put me in one of those guest cottages?"

Edda Mae pulled on a neon-pink hooded slicker

over her curlers and robe. "We had the exterminator in this afternoon. Ain't nobody staying in those rooms until they've been aired out and wiped clean. And we can't start that until tomorrow."

Frowning, Edda Mae looked Vince up and down, then handed him a small purple umbrella with pink polka dots. "Which is why you'll be sleeping with your wife tonight."

CHAPTER FOUR

"I THOUGHT married people lived together."

"Most of them do." Jill had finished reading Teddy a chapter of his book, raising her voice to be heard above the rain beating on their roof. Now her throat felt scratchy.

Eyes averted, Teddy plucked at his comforter. It was lime green and matched one of the walls she and Teddy had painted. "Are *you* going to live together?"

"No." She'd been surprised to see that Vince still wore his wedding ring. Because of Craig, Jill used hers like a shield. Vince had no reason to wear his. "We don't have a marriage like other people. In fact, I don't know how long we're going to stay married. I doubt Vince will come back."

More plucking by Teddy.

"What's bothering you?"

"Can't we keep him? As my dad?"

"No! He's a person, not a pet."

"Everybody else has a dad but me." Teddy gave Jill his best puppy-dog eyes.

"You know that's not true."

Teddy tugged at the comforter some more. "I think I'll go to sleep now."

"Teddy?"

"I'm really tired." He rolled over to face the wall, leaving Jill no choice but to turn off the light and wish him good-night.

As soon as she closed Teddy's door someone knocked on the front one, followed by a muffled, "It's me. Edda Mae."

"What's wrong? Did the power go out in your cottage?" It was really storming now and there was no reason for Edda Mae to be up. As quickly as she could, Jill undid the old chain, flipped back the dead bolt and turned the lock on the handle.

"Surprise," Vince said, looking windblown and more handsome than he had a right to, hugging the rail as Edda Mae traipsed past him down the stairs.

"Edda Mae?" Jill's cheeks heated. She should have made sure Vince left thirty minutes ago.

"Storm's here. Remember your manners," Edda Mae called.

The wind rushed up the stairwell, past Vince and his duffel, dancing around Jill's bare feet.

"Should I walk her back?" Vince glanced after Jill's meddling surrogate mother, a small purple umbrella clutched in his hand.

"Did she pull that frail-old-woman act on you? She's steadier on her feet than a mountain goat and just as stubborn. She'll be fine." At least until the morning when Jill gave her a piece of her mind.

Vince nodded absently. Neither of them spoke. The rain continued to pour.

"I should go," Vince said eventually. Yet he stood there staring. At Jill.

For about two seconds, Jill considered making Vince drive in the storm. Water gushed out of the rain gutter below. The route down the mountain was treacherous; and anything could happen on a night like this—mud slides, hidden potholes, unexpected pools of water. It wouldn't take much for someone unfamiliar with the road driving a sexy little sports car a bit too fast to end up stuck in a ditch. Or worse.

"I suppose Edda Mae told you about our cottages. All I've got to offer you is the couch." A lumpy, short couch.

"That'll do." Without setting eyes on it, Vince flashed Jill his dimple.

It was such a rare sight—that dimple—that it took her back to their wedding day. Jill was frozen, spellbound.

"Jill?" Vince gestured toward the living room. "Can I come in?"

Jill stumbled to the side to let Vince pass and escaped to collect a clean sheet and blanket. She took a pillow from her own bed. When she returned Vince was examining the wall where her framed photos were arranged. He'd removed his tie and unbuttoned his dress shirt. The T-shirt beneath fit him snugly and Jill paused in the hallway, struck with the urge to run her hands over the soft cotton, something she'd done many times to her shadow husband. But never to the real thing. She wouldn't have the courage.

"Where was this one taken?" Vince straightened a picture of Teddy. With a grin as wide as Texas, Teddy stood on the bank of a river holding a golf-ball-size piece of fool's gold, looking like he was trying to convince Jill he'd struck it rich.

Clutching the bedding tighter, Jill propelled herself past Vince. "The Mokelumne River. It's not far from here."

"Looks like you had a great time that day. My family doesn't have pictures like this. I'm not sure why..." He wandered farther down the wall of photos.

Jill experienced a pang of guilt. Vince had mentioned earlier he'd wanted to be a part of Teddy's life. He'd said as much before they'd gotten married, too. Why was he so attached to a child he hadn't fathered when she...?

Jill began folding and tucking the bedding into the creases of the couch. Now she was feeling guilty about the couch, too. "This wasn't designed for someone to sleep on. It's short."

"And narrow," he added, staring at it.

She'd finished with the linens, but she couldn't look at Vince and her mobility problem had returned. Her feet were leaden, weighted down by myriad emotions—desire, shame, confusion—all of them unwelcome. "But at least you'll be safe and dry tomorrow morning."

Vince sighed. "So I can be on my way."

"Yes." So that her life could return to normal.

"And you can try to derail the tribe's plan for a casino." There was no hint of recrimination in his voice. "Is Shady Oak that successful on its own?"

"I'm just breaking even." It was painful to admit.

Jill couldn't quite bring herself to look at Vince. "The key to Shady Oak's success is in our luxurious accommodations and isolation. Wireless service doesn't work here. Without the daily distractions of e-mail and cell-phone calls, my clients can focus and be more productive." Her parents had alternately complained and praised that aspect of Shady Oak on one of their rare visits. "Edda Mae is a wonderful storyteller. She has a Native American story with a moral to fit every situation. We promise at least one story each booking."

Vince was frowning at his BlackBerry. "And the vacation homes?"

"The plan *I* support for growth is to build a gated community of luxury vacation homes on a first-class golf course. The casino doesn't benefit Railroad Stop residents equally—the profits will go to the tribe."

His head shot up with the oddest expression, a mixture of wariness and disbelief. "It's an *Indian* casino. What about taxes? Jobs? Which will provide you with more?"

"Long-term, jobs would be a wash, I think. A successful casino might bring in more in tax revenue in the long run. But you'd have to gamble on it being special enough to be a destination, and 'special' costs money. There are other casinos closer to civilization in the valley that are an easier drive."

Vince peered at her intently, then laughed. "Nice try. I think I'll wait for Arnie's projections."

Unexpectedly disappointed that Vince didn't trust her, Jill bit her lip and let her gaze fall to the floor.

Thunder rumbled overhead, filling the awkward void between them.

"You never got around to telling me why you left me," Vince said gently.

Jill's head shot up. "You accused me—"

"Let's not circle back to that." There was no anger in Vince's expression, only compassion. This was the Vince she'd married.

"I'm not proud I left, Vince. You offered me something I wasn't ready to take." Jill's voice was brittle from years of guilt. "We were kids ourselves. After what happened I couldn't—"

"I would have waited. I told you on our wedding night—"

Hugging herself, Jill stepped back. "You don't understand. It wasn't about us *sleeping…*" She choked on the word. Jill willed herself to keep it together. "You don't…I… I left Las Vegas because I was ashamed."

"No one knew about Craig but you and me."

"I'm not talking about Craig," Jill said, tightening her arms about herself. "I was ashamed that I couldn't be sure…that I didn't know… You had no doubts, but I was going to have a baby that was created from an act of violence. I wasn't sure I could love it."

It was a rare occasion that left Vince speechless.

"I knew what it was like to grow up without love. I came second to our family casino. I couldn't do that to another child," Jill whispered. "And if you loved the baby and I couldn't, our marriage would have been a terrible mistake." A far bigger mistake than it had been.

"You could have said something," Vince returned gruffly. "I would have understood."

"You would have tried to convince me I'd learn to love the baby." Vince could coerce the devil if he wanted to. Once on a class field trip to an amusement park, he'd persuaded Jill to try a crazy-scary roller coaster. Her stomach still flipped at the memory. "I was getting over the shock of what happened. By the time I realized how I felt, we were married."

"You would have given Teddy up for adoption?" She'd never seen Vince so dumbfounded.

Jill nodded. She forced her arms to relax, brought an image of Teddy as a baby to mind and found herself smiling. "But I loved Teddy from the second I laid eyes on him."

"Then why didn't you come back?"

"Because you deserved so much more out of life than a broken woman and another man's child." Drained, Jill wanted nothing more than to collapse on a chair.

"At least you were right about one thing," he said unforgivingly.

Jill bristled. She'd come clean. She didn't need Vince's bitterness. "I've got a long day tomorrow. Good night."

Those two words rekindled the intimacy she'd felt with him earlier. Jill edged toward the hall, eyes on the floor, torn between wanting to slug Vince and needing to be held by him.

"Isn't this funny?" Vince said softly.

Jill's head snapped up.

"You and me under the same roof. Me on the couch. Déjà vu." His dark eyes hinted at old hurts. "You don't plan to run out on me in the middle of the night, do you?"

Jill's chin came up a notch. "Teddy's asleep. Down the hall." She wasn't about to leave her son. This was her home.

"He must be a sound sleeper to snooze through all this." Vince's half smile wasn't apologetic or rueful. It was...

Vince couldn't be thinking...

Oh, yes, he could. He'd been the bad boy all the high-school girls whispered about with longing in their voices. Rumors abounded about Vince, rumors based on what someone told someone else about some unknown girl at some other high school and her lost virtue.

"That'll be enough of that," Jill said as matter-of-factly as she could manage without quite looking him in the eye. The last thing she wanted was for Vince to see how he unsettled her.

On shaky legs, Jill retreated to her bedroom and shut herself in, his deep laughter following her. She climbed into the dormer window and leaned her forehead against the cool glass, striped with tears from the storm. Vince had always managed to be one step ahead of her. She might kick Vince out tomorrow, but he'd be around, studying her, trying to anticipate her next move to block his casino. She'd need more than garishly painted signs to stop Vince and Arnie.

She should be angry or anxious. Yet her heart beat faster knowing her husband was in her home, sleeping between sheets that had touched her skin.

She should never have created the fantasy Vince, the ideal husband. The real Vince wasn't perfect. He had a hair-trigger temper and he loved the trappings of success, the energy and excitement of Vegas. Whereas Jill was often uncomfortable in her own skin and content living her life behind a security fence.

So why did she still find Vince so compelling?

Jill stroked the angles of the diamond on her wedding ring, but for once it gave her no comfort.

CHUCKLING, VINCE PLUMPED up the pillow Jill had given him and lay down on the couch. Despite the surprising revelation about why she'd left, Jill amused him.

Few women he ran across in his life did that nowadays. In fact, he couldn't remember the last time being with a woman without having sex had been so much fun.

If he was a cat, she'd be the mouse. She'd given too much away tonight, providing Vince with information he could use to his advantage. And she'd always been a soft touch. It wouldn't be long before Vince had Jill supporting his efforts in Railroad Stop. He wouldn't let their past and his fondness for her stand in the way.

There was just enough light outside to cast liquid shadows on the ceiling. Something hard poked his hip. Vince shifted and reached beneath the sheet to find a button on the cushion. He edged closer to the back of the couch only to encounter another in the middle of his back. Edda Mae's love seat was starting to look better and better. Through trial and error Vince found a way to avoid the buttons, certain that his position on the couch had some fancy name in yoga.

A light and flowery aroma filled his nostrils. He turned his head and drank in the smell of Jill from the soft cotton pillowcase. He'd only been close to a handful of people in his life—his grandparents, his best friend, Sam, and for a few weeks, Jill. For years, he'd taken her abandonment personally. Jill's leaving had never made sense, until now.

He'd understood Jill from the first day of kindergarten. While other kids were walked to class by their moms or dropped off by dads in luxury SUVs, Vince stepped out of a large black Town Car driven by his family's chauffeur. But at least the windows were so dark that no one could tell his mom wasn't inside.

Jill didn't have it so lucky. On good days she hopped out of dented old cars driven by someone in a white shirt with a name tag. Sometimes during the off-season the hotel shuttle bus pulled into the school's circular driveway—social suicide.

And yet Jill kept smiling, kept trying to fit in, not that the kids ever really let her. Vince didn't fit in out of necessity. It was safer alone. That way he didn't have to explain anything. In school he'd kept his mouth shut and his head down, until he discovered that the bruises that occasionally showed up on his face in junior high gave him a bad-ass reputation that guaranteed others kept their distance. Besides, his dad always apologized when he sobered up.

Vince's gaze drifted to the shadows of a bookshelf where he'd seen a photo of Jill in front of a Christmas tree, cradling Teddy and wearing a guarded smile. Two weeks after Senior Ditch Day she'd bolted out of physics class to throw up and found Vince waiting outside the girls' bathroom door. He'd driven her to a coffee shop, fed her toast and listened to her babble about her parents and how they'd never really loved their only child.

Vince understood Jill, all right. Now if he could just make her see things his way….

"EDDA MAE, what are you doing here?" Jill whispered when she returned to her apartment the next morning. She'd risen at dawn to find the sky clear again and had spray-painted NO CASINO! on all the signs.

"I'm makin' breakfast." Edda Mae smiled from Jill's sunny kitchen as if everything was right with the world, but Jill wasn't fooled. Edda Mae was here to see if Jill and Vince had slept together.

"He's still here," Teddy said in a low voice, pointing at Vince asleep on the couch. "Are you sure we can't keep him?"

Edda Mae laughed softly while Jill shushed the two of them.

Vince's long legs spilled over the end of the couch while Moonbeam curled in the crook of his arm. Vince slept as if he hadn't a care in the world, but Jill had tossed and turned all night wondering why Vince had come to Railroad Stop—it couldn't have been a coincidence—and wondering what she was going to do to about the casino.

Teddy came to stand beside Jill and they stared at their houseguest. Jill wanted to do damage with her fingers to Vince's tamed, dark hair. Nobody should look that good in the morning wearing yesterday's slacks and a baggy, long-sleeved T-shirt, especially a man who was trying to turn her world upside down.

One of Vince's toes twitched. His feet were big and sturdy, the kind that moved purposefully forward when confrontation loomed. Jill was almost envious. Her feet were small and always seemed to back away.

When Teddy poked Vince's foot with his finger, Vince jerked awake, black eyes bleary and ringed with dark circles, as if he'd tried more than a polite sip of Edda Mae's whiskey last night. Moonbeam growled and Vince grimaced.

A smile tugged at Jill's lips.

"A little help here." Head straining to one side, Vince pointed to the protesting dog with his free hand.

A boyish giggle filled the air.

Edda Mae poked her head out of the kitchen. "You'll need more food now that you've got an extra mouth to feed."

"If you're determined to keep him, take him to your place." Jill removed Moonbeam from Vince's chest, depositing the pooch in Teddy's arms.

"Thanks." Vince's intense gaze seemed bent on capturing her own, but Jill wasn't to be trapped.

She scurried over to the kitchen where bacon sizzled in a pan, pausing to wash her hands at the sink, which gave her a view of the living room.

"I told you she gets up early, boy," Edda Mae said, snapping a green kitchen towel at Vince's knee before trundling back to the kitchen without an ounce of remorse in her expression.

Matchmaking. Busybody. Traitor.

Edda Mae met Jill's narrowed gaze and shrugged.

"I feel like a pretzel," Vince grumbled as he pushed himself upright in fits and starts.

Teddy grinned from ear to ear as he watched Vince unfold himself from the furniture. Gathering Moonbeam closer with one hand, Teddy pointed to Vince's chest with the other. "You have dog drool on your shirt."

Vince spread the white cotton with both hands. "What the...?" He sank back onto the love seat, thumbs rubbing temples.

"You gave him whiskey?" With a huff of disgust, Jill searched her cabinet for some aspirin. Everyone in Railroad Stop knew Edda Mae's homemade whiskey was more powerful than jet fuel and just as deadly.

Vince was clueless. Yet another difference between her fantasy Vince and the real McCoy.

"I did no such thing." Edda Mae used a fork to turn over the bacon strips.

"I turned her down." Beyond the occasional shoulder-and-neck roll, Vince wasn't moving. He barely acknowledged Jill when she offered him a glass of water and two aspirin tablets.

"Teddy, wash up for breakfast." Jill turned her back on Vince and went to set her small dining table. "Once you've fed Vince, Edda Mae, he'll be on his way."

"He's a bit of a pretty boy. Don't you think he might like to shower and shave before you send him down the hill?" Edda Mae took eggs out of the refrigerator.

"We're not running a bathhouse," Jill countered, more than a little uncomfortable with the idea of Vince naked in her shower. "Remember him? He's the enemy."

"He's no such thing," Edda Mae pooh-poohed her, then frowned and stared at Vince. "He's so pretty, in fact, he might be one of those men who like men. I could be wrong but—"

"You're wrong," Vince growled. "Not that I have anything against men who like men. I'm just not one of them."

Edda Mae didn't look convinced.

Jill tried not to smile. "He and Arnie want to build a casino, remember?"

"I want a golf course," Teddy said, grinning at Vince. "I'd like to play golf if I had someone to teach me."

"Have you looked at his face?" Edda Mae continued. "That's a face you can trust."

Jill rolled her eyes.

"Come on, Mom. You did marry him." Teddy came into the kitchen and put Moonbeam down so he could wash his hands. "There must be something about him you like."

Jill didn't want to remember.

Prancing expectantly around Edda Mae's ankles, the little dog began to yap.

"Moonbeam's cranky this morning. She's out of food," Edda Mae announced.

Never a patient dog, Moonbeam barked louder while Edda Mae apologized to her for forgetting to buy dog food and Teddy rooted in the pantry for something Moonbeam could eat, all the while claiming Moonbeam should have bacon for breakfast.

"Excuse me." Scowling, Vince entered the kitchen, which suddenly seemed too crowded to Jill, but Edda Mae, Teddy and Moonbeam didn't seem to notice how much space a big, angry man could take up. *"Excuse me!"*

Everyone fell silent, until Moonbeam realized it was Vince who was shouting and she still hadn't been fed. She returned to her protest.

"Back off, looney dog," Vince growled right back at her.

Moonbeam sat down and gazed up at Vince as if he were about to give her a piece of the bacon that crackled in the pan above her. Jill shouldn't have been surprised. Vince had always been able to get girls to eat out of his hand.

"In the past twenty-four hours I've been lost in the woods and kicked out of this place, after which I nearly mowed down an innocent bystander, was threatened by a poofy mouse with fangs and slept on what has got to be the most uncomfortable couch in the state of California." He glared at each of them in turn.

First at Teddy. "No, the dog is *not* getting bacon for breakfast even if I have to drive into town to buy her kibble."

Then at Edda Mae. "No, I am *not* a pretty boy. I've been in my share of fights and served in the war. I've got scars. That doesn't mean I don't want to have a shower and a shave, but…"

And here he turned to Jill. "No, I will *not* be leaving when I'm done eating bacon and eggs. We have issues that need to be discussed—including, but not limited to, the state of our marriage and your objections to my casino."

This was it. He was going to end their farcical union right here in front of Edda Mae and Teddy. Jill held her breath.

But Vince didn't ask for a divorce. He shook his head and turned away.

Filling her lungs with air, Jill slouched against the counter, knowing she shouldn't be so relieved. She needed to pull on her big-girl panties and tell Vince she wanted a divorce, rather than wait until he brought it up.

Vince spun back around. "And I'd appreciate it if you wouldn't talk about me as if I wasn't here, especially before I've had my first cup of coffee." Chin up, Vince dared any of them to challenge him.

Jill knew she should. At the very least she had to make it clear that he wasn't spending the night on her couch again. Vince had the power to shred the safety net she'd created. He'd already started. But words eluded her.

"Looney Moony." Teddy giggled, pleased with his rhyme.

CHAPTER FIVE

EDDA MAE REMEMBERED she'd left Moonbeam's kibble in the Shady Oak kitchen when she was filling the shelves last week. Vince offered to go downstairs and retrieve it—being more curious than he wanted to admit about this luxury retreat of Jill's—but apparently he needed a key and someone who knew the security code. Since Edda Mae was cooking Jill suggested Teddy take him. She didn't seem to want to be alone with Vince or divulge the code.

"Why do elephants paint their toenails red?" Teddy asked, skipping down the stairs ahead of Vince.

"I don't know," Vince said absently, still trying to figure out Jill's state of mind.

"So they can hide in a strawberry patch." Teddy swung around the bottom stair, grinning at Vince. "Get it? Their toenails are big and round and red like strawberries."

Vince groaned. He'd forgotten how truly bad a young boy's jokes could be. But he couldn't resist trying one of his own. After all, telling bad jokes was part of being a kid. "Have you ever seen an elephant's toenails?"

Teddy shook his head.

"Those would be some mammoth strawberries."

A small crease appeared between Teddy's eyebrows.

With a put-upon sigh, Vince rolled his eyes. "Get it? Mammoth? Elephant?"

"Oh." Teddy giggled. "Why do elephants hide in strawberry patches?"

After considering for a moment, Vince gave up. "I don't know."

Teddy's lower lip thrust out in disappointment. "Take a guess. Mom hardly ever guesses."

If that wasn't a challenge, Vince didn't know what was. "Because they eat straw?"

"No-o. So they can jump out and stomp on people." Teddy waited for Vince to laugh before he rounded a corner. He stopped in front of an unimposing door, flipped up the lid of a plastic box installed on the wall and keyed in a series of numbers. "Why do elephants stomp on people?"

"To make people whine…wine?" It was a stretch, but Teddy wanted him to guess.

"No! That's why they play squash." Teddy plodded around, his right arm curling as if it were an elephant's trunk while he made *mmfffttt* noises. Then he grinned up at Vince expectantly.

"Ha, ha. Your friends must think you're a laugh a minute."

Teddy's smile crumpled. "My skunk jokes are better."

"I can't wait, but—" Vince held up a hand before Teddy could launch into his stinky repertoire "—let's find the dog food first. I can hear that looney beast complaining from here."

Tilting his head, Teddy paused and then chuckled as he searched through the set of keys on the ring Jill had given him. "Yep, she's still complaining."

Once Teddy found the right key, the door opened on silent hinges into a huge kitchen with a dark hardwood floor. Black marble counters over oak cabinets made a *U* around the room. Pots and pans hung from the ceiling over a large center island. There were two of everything—stoves, refrigerators, microwaves, all shiny new stainless steel which must have set Jill back plenty. There was a Dutch door opposite the entrance they'd come through and a high counter with shutters on top that he guessed served as a pass-through to the dining room.

While Teddy rooted around in the cupboards, Vince pushed open the Dutch door and walked into the dining room. He whistled once in appreciation as he let the door swish closed behind him. Jill had gone all out here. This was no summer camp. The room was way more lavish than the simple apartment above it.

Vince had been to more than his share of luxury hotels. She'd obviously taken inspiration from high-end lodges. The dining room was a showcase of polished floors, upscale wooden tables and saloon chairs and exquisite chandeliers, with the centerpiece a grand stone fireplace next to a bank of windows that looked out over a porch to the gently rolling valley below. The view was breathtaking.

Jill hadn't exaggerated Shady Oak's potential. It could be a huge success. If the individual rooms were anything like this, she'd be booked years in advance. Vince's mind cranked through what else she'd need—advertising, more staff, weekend getaway deals with the local casino.

"Found it." Teddy flung the door open, bumping Vince with it. "Let's go."

Vince followed the boy out, waiting while he locked up and reset the alarm. "Are the cottages like this?"

Teddy shrugged, clearly not interested. "Mom says the cottages turned out way better."

His curiosity piqued, Vince stared at the cabins closest to the dining hall.

Teddy tugged on Vince's shirt. "Hey. What do you get when you cross a skunk with a bear?"

"A zebra?" That was a stretch.

"*Winnie the Pew!* Here, carry this." The Prince of Bad Jokes handed Vince the small bag of dog food, then raced off. "Last one upstairs is a rotten egg."

"TELL ME ABOUT your family, Vince," Edda Mae commanded when they'd all sat down to eat breakfast.

"Edda Mae." Jill cast a nervous glance at Vince. During their short engagement Jill's few questions about Vince's mom and dad had been met with silent shrugs. His parents hadn't attended their private ceremony. She doubted they'd been invited.

Teddy set his milk down. Out of habit, Jill swabbed his milk mustache away while he swatted at her hand.

But Vince answered smoothly, "There's not much to tell. I'm an only child."

"Men," Edda Mae huffed. "I need more than that. I want to know what kind of family you came from, how you were raised..." *What kind of person you are.* Edda Mae didn't have to elaborate. Jill had firsthand experience with Edda Mae's conversation-interrogation tactics.

Vince was too well mannered to frown, but he was buttering his toast like he was drawing a line in the sand, a boundary that said Off Limits. As if Teddy sensed the tension among the grown-ups, the only thing moving in his region of the table were his eyes, swiveling from adult to adult in wide-eyed fascination.

"For instance…," Edda Mae began when it was obvious Vince wasn't going to be forthcoming with any information.

"Vince lived with his grandparents in Las Vegas when he was younger," Jill interrupted, nearly spilling her milk in her haste to prevent World War III from breaking out in her dining room. "How are your grandparents?"

With enviable grace, Vince set the knife down silently on the edge of the butter tray. "My grandmother was in a car accident a year and a half ago. She's been in a coma ever since."

"Oh, dear Lord," Edda Mae said, her fork clattering to her plate.

Jill laid her hand on Vince's upper arm. Although he didn't move, his whole body seemed to tense at her touch. He stared at Jill's hand so intently she drew it away in confusion and covered her surprise by asking, "How is your grandfather?" The few times she'd met the legendary Aldo Patrizio she'd been both charmed and intimidated.

"My grandfather hasn't been the same since," Vince admitted in a husky voice. "He's…well, he's finding it difficult."

"So you've been helping him with the business," Jill said, trying not to frown as she pondered Vince's reaction to her touch. She must have imagined the desire in his eyes last night, which was all good. Theirs was meant to be a platonic relationship. Jill tapped Teddy's plate with one finger, reminding him to eat.

"And your parents?" Edda Mae asked. "Are they helping your grandfather while you're away?"

"No. The only interest they have in the business is what their share will be when my grandfather dies." Vince examined his toast intently, as if the fate of the world depended on where he took his first bite.

Edda Mae gasped. "You don't mean that."

"Yes, I do. Not everyone is capable of loving someone." Vince crunched on his toast.

Jill's heart went out to Vince. She knew how desolate life could be with parents who evaluated rather than loved.

But then she wondered.

Was he talking about her?

"TEDDY IS LIKE one of my own grandkids." Edda Mae chatted pleasantly to Vince as she handed him a dripping plate to dry. Apparently his confession about his parents hadn't destroyed her opinion of him.

Unlike Jill, who'd treated him coolly ever since she'd placed her hand over the scar on his arm at breakfast. Could she have felt the twisted, hardened skin through the thin cotton of his T-shirt? The few people who'd seen his scar wanted to know how he got it. Vince didn't satisfy their interest other than to say, "The war."

"I tell everyone I have three grandchildren," Edda Mae went on. "My daughter, Francie, and her two girls live near Fresno. It takes nearly four hours to get there from here—unless Jill drives."

"She's still heavy on the pedal, huh?" Vince smiled, remembering the one time he'd let Jill take his sports car for a spin before they got married. Jill had a way of accelerating that gave her passengers whiplash. He'd always suspected Jill was as impatient and impetuous as he was. She just hid it better until she got behind the wheel.

Edda Mae chuckled, the rich sound drawing him further into the Norman Rockwell–like moment—no servants walking on silent feet, no assistants slipping notes, no managers reporting problems on the casino floor.

Out of the corner of his eye Vince saw Teddy sprawled on his belly reading a book. Moonbeam was curled next to him, full of kibble. With half an ear Vince listened to Jill book a group for a stay in January, her tone calm and reassuring. Vince knew if he turned around he'd find her worrying the end of a pencil with her teeth, so at odds with the confidence in her voice.

Jill's household was nothing like the one Vince had grown up in. And yet, it felt like home.

"Too bad your daughter lives so far away," Vince said to Edda Mae, reaching for a dry dish towel.

"Francie wanted to go to college. Afterward she wasn't interested in running Shady Oak and there weren't any other jobs here for someone with a degree in finance. I miss her, but—" with a determined grip, Edda Mae wrestled the heavy frying pan into the sink "—what can I do?"

If he succeeded, if there was a casino in Railroad Stop, maybe Edda Mae's daughter could move back.

A casino needed more financial experts than a golf course did. As soon as Jill was off the phone Vince was going to point that out to her.

"You sold the business to Jill. You're free to go to Fresno, right?" Vince reached in front of Edda Mae to put the four plates in the cupboard above the sink. "Jill seems to know what she's doing."

Just as Jill hung up the phone, Edda Mae's grip on the frying pan slipped and it bounced against the stainless-steel sink with a bang.

"Gun! Shooter!" Vince was never sure how he got the warning past his parched throat.

Sam lifted his M16 and began firing.

Yap-yap-yap-yap.

Vince frowned. Dogs usually ran for cover at the first sound of gunfire.

He blinked.

Moonbeam was on Teddy's back, yelping her displeasure at something.

"Hey. Ow." Teddy squirmed until the little dog leaped off, still barking.

"Darn and double darn," Edda Mae said, taking in her soaked blouse and jeans and then the water around her feet. "Moonbeam, hush."

Dogzilla ignored her owner.

Everything was chaotically the same. Vince began breathing. No one had noticed his descent into the past.

And then he saw Jill staring at him.

Unwilling to be her lab specimen, Vince snapped off two paper towels and knelt to attack the puddles. He didn't want Edda Mae to slip and fall, plus it gave him an excuse to duck out of Jill's line of sight and examine the pretty blue linoleum. "Don't move, Edda Mae. I've got it."

Jill scooped up Moonbeam and shushed her, bringing much needed quiet to the room. Then she ruined it by coming to stand in the kitchen entry.

Vince braced himself.

"A man who does dishes *and* floors?" Jill asked in a voice laced with sarcasm. "I thought venture capitalists were clueless about stuff like that."

"One of my first jobs was washing dishes in the Sicilian's coffee shop. What was yours? Guard duty at the photocopy machine?" Vince let his tone convey a level of disdain equal to hers. You could say all you wanted about the Patrizios, but they had a strong work ethic.

"Lucky," Teddy said. "My job's cleaning toilets." He took over the computer as soon as Jill vacated the desk chair.

Cradling soggy, dripping paper towels, Vince got to his feet, but he avoided looking Jill in the eye. Maybe she hadn't noticed he'd transported himself to another time.

But what if she had? She'd think he was crazy, which would present a huge obstacle for Vince to overcome here in Railroad Stop.

"Jill, where is your mop?" Edda Mae glanced around the kitchen.

"Between the refrigerator and the cupboard. The same place you kept it for years." Jill stared at Edda Mae. "Are you having a senior moment?"

"Oh." Edda Mae chuckled as she reached for it. "Well, I am a senior, so I guess I'm entitled to one now and then."

Jill set the dog on the floor. She stepped closer to Vince, concern in her eyes. "Are you okay?"

Like he was going to say no? Diversionary tactics were called for.

"I need to ask you something. Alone." Vince claimed Jill's arm and steered her toward the door. There was no way he was letting Jill ask him questions, much less ask them in front of Teddy and Edda Mae. Besides, if he proposed a closer business relationship with his casino, Jill might see how advantageous the deal would be to both of them.

Moonbeam skittered out of their way.

Downstairs, Jill stepped out of Vince's grasp and led him across the gravel parking lot toward the garage, the sky a gemlike blue above the towering pines ahead of her. "I know what you're going to say, what you're going to ask me."

What the—? She was a mind reader now? "Do you?"

"It should be easy," Jill continued, not looking back, the natural red streaks in her hair glinting in the sun.

"Of course it is. As long as we agree," Vince said with relief. Jill must have come to the same conclusion he had this morning when he saw Shady Oak's dining room. They could both benefit if they worked together.

They walked past the garage. Beneath the overhang the boards they'd painted last night leaned against the wall.

Jill led Vince up a path farther away from the building, her jeans snug across her hips. Her hourglass figure would have most men itching to trace those curves with both hands. Most men. Not Vince.

He'd become immune to her charms the night she'd walked out of his life. All that was left now was a detached appreciation of her figure.

"Did you bring the paperwork?" Jill asked. "You must have been thinking about this for a long time."

"It's too soon." A contract with the tribe would need to include specific financial agreements and obligations. He and Arnie were still talking big-picture numbers as they danced around approvals.

Vince saw that words had been painted on the boards, but from this angle he couldn't read them. Jill and Teddy must have gotten up early. Another step, maybe two…

"It's been more than ten years, Vince."

Now Vince could see the big, bold red letters. He stopped, staring at the spray-painted phrase—NO CASINO. This was a problem. An amateurish, grass-roots problem, to be sure. Still, if Jill teamed up with the mayor Arnie had warned Vince about, she'd be trouble. Vince didn't have time for trouble.

"I helped you paint those," Vince said, jabbing his finger at the signs. "I thought you said it was Teddy's school project."

Jill shook her head twice, so slowly her ponytail barely moved. "You assumed—"

"Oh, come on, Jill. You could have set me straight last night." Vince glanced back at the painted boards, torn between the need to shake Jill and kiss her senseless.

Wait a minute. Kiss Jill? Vince frowned. Jill was maddening. Jill was amusing. He stared at her.

Yes, he wanted to kiss her.

"What?" Jill's brow creased.

"Nothing." Kissing would be a big mistake. He wanted to bring her into the casino deal, not scare her away.

"I hope you're not arguing with that nice man again," Edda Mae called, crossing the lot to her cottage.

"You're talking about me as if I'm not here." Frowning, Vince swung around. "Again."

"Apologies." Edda Mae laughed, Moonbeam a poofy white ball bouncing at her feet. "But you had your coffee."

Shaking his head, Vince returned his attention to his wife, who looked nervous. "What were you going to ask me before?"

"I…uhh…" Now that he'd seen the signs, Vince knew bringing Jill into the casino deal was a long shot. "It was probably the same thing I was going to ask you."

Jill walked up the hill away from Vince. "I meant to do this a long time ago."

"What?" Vince's gaze had swung back to the boards. He'd helped her paint them. He'd helped her—

"Divorce you."

What the—!

Vince spun around, his knees jerking unsteadily as his world tilted and fell out of focus so that all he could see was his long-lost wife. Jill hadn't come to her senses. She'd totally lost her mind. Divorce her? Why? This marriage was the perfect setup.

"Vince?" Jill circled the small rise, the sun casting filtered light through the tall trees behind her.

Vince couldn't find his voice.

"You're not divorcing me?" There was a wobbly note of hope underlying her words.

"No," Vince blurted. "Why would I?"

"Maybe because we're not really married?" Jill gave him a soft, sad smile, looking more like the girl in school who never quite fit in than an accomplished businesswoman. "You live your life and I live mine."

"Yes. It's perfect." He was starting to sound like a total idiot. But Vegas was full of women looking for a meal ticket, and without his wedding ring his life would be…complicated. Or at least more complicated than it already was.

"It's not a marriage, Vince."

"Is this about money?"

"I don't want your money." Jill's smile became more animated. "Well, that's not quite true. When you sell the house my parents gave us, I'd like my share."

Vince took a few steps closer so that he could see her face, gauge if she'd fallen for another man. "Is there someone else?"

"No," she said much too quickly.

"Because you have carte blanche. I know I certainly have."

It was the wrong thing to say. Jill crossed her arms over her chest and raised her eyebrows.

"You thought I'd been a monk all these years?" Vince could tell by the way Jill worried her lip with her teeth that she hoped he had. It went against everything he'd once felt to hurt her but, "I refuse to feel guilty. *You* left *me*."

Jill studied him, judged him. Vince's hands fisted at his sides.

Then Jill sighed. "Why?"

"Why what?"

"I don't know," she said. "Why did you marry me? Why didn't you divorce me?"

He ground his teeth. She didn't understand. "Jill—"

She waved a hand in his direction. "Clearly, you don't want to be married."

"I wear my ring, don't I?" Vince didn't know where his anger was coming from. He was nearly shouting.

"Why keep it on? So you can pick up girls who aren't looking for anything more than a one-nighter?"

The admission broke free. "Yes. You know better than anyone that I'm not cut out for this love business. My parents sure as hell didn't love me. My dad thought a good backhand to the head was an appropriate father-son greeting. And my grandfather...well, whatever he once felt for me is long gone. I know who I am, Jill. I know what I have to offer."

"Sex." The word sounded foreign coming off Jill's lips.

"Guilty as charged." Vince waited for Jill to close in for the kill. He was scum. He deserved it, probably more so because he wanted to kiss her. "Damn it, Jill. If we're ending this thing, we'll do it the same way we started." With a kiss. Only this time it wouldn't be G-rated.

Capturing Jill's gaze, Vince moved another few feet up the path. The Jill he'd married would have made an excuse and scurried away.

News flash: Jill wasn't backing off.

They were going to kiss. Vince could see from the widening of Jill's blue eyes that she knew it, too.

CHAPTER SIX

JILL'S HEART POUNDED, urging her to flee, to hide the warmth creeping up her neck.

Stupid, stupid fantasies.

But the rest of her railed, insisting she demand Vince leave. He must think her a real piece of work. What kind of woman left her husband on their wedding night and didn't annul the marriage right away and then waited—after he'd admitted his marriage vows meant nothing to him—for him to kiss her goodbye?

Vince stared at her without speaking as he advanced. And yet, Jill swore she could hear his thoughts. He wanted to know everything—from Jill's reason for marrying him to her excuse for staying away after she discovered she adored Teddy to why she never divorced him. He'd listen, because that's what he'd always done for her. He'd listen to Jill whether he stood in the chilly September sunshine in dress slacks and a white sodden T-shirt or they sat on the hearth in the dining room with a fire blazing behind them or lay in bed—

No. That was her fantasy Vince. This Vince was hungry and after instant gratification. He stalked toward her, his long strides reminiscent of the proud boy who'd survived on the fringe of high-school society. But where he'd been lanky as a teenager, he was solid now with a broad chest and muscular arms that could crush a woman to him whether she wanted that intimacy or not.

Jill was unable to pull her gaze away from Vince's lips. It was a crime for a man to have such a perfect mouth. There'd been no one since Vince's kiss sealed their vows. Her wedding ring ensured that.

When Jill didn't argue, Vince paused and cocked an eyebrow, sending another unwanted, heated signal her body couldn't ignore.

Get a grip. If not for yourself, then for Teddy.

That jolted Jill's brain back into defense mode. "This is not how I pictured us meeting after all these years."

Vince frowned. "You've been hiding up here waiting for me to serve you divorce papers?" He ambled a few feet closer, close enough to touch Jill with an extended arm. Close enough for her to sink her fingers into his thick, dark hair.

And have him flinch at her touch as he'd done at breakfast? She was nothing to him. Undoubtedly she was misreading the entire situation. Vince was here to wreak havoc on Railroad Stop and to do so he had to put her off balance. There was no way he could send out those smoking sexy vibes unconsciously. He was messing with her libido, all right. He could probably see the infrared stamp on her forehead that said *sexually repressed, yet undeniably curious.* And it *was* curiosity about Vince.

Jill backed up a step and then another. She had enough problems of her own without trying to figure out what was going on in Vince's head. "It makes sense. You should be free to pursue whatever... whoever you want."

"Come on. Haven't you ever wondered what it would be like to kiss me? Now's your last chance." Vince advanced on Jill again, slowly. "Prove to me you're ready to move on."

How did you do that after being date-raped? She'd been a willing participant at first. Craig hadn't been able to stop. What man could at that point? No. It was safer to sleep alone. Jill clumped clumsily to the edge of the tree line. They were out of sight of the main buildings now. Her heart hammered. "I've lived without you for ten years. I think I've proved I can do it."

"That's not what I meant." Vince kept coming toward her.

Ten years ago she would have held up a hand to indicate that was close enough and he would have respected her wishes. He'd known she was nervous around men. Why wasn't he stopping? "Vince?"

He halted at her question. Two steps above Vince on the trail, Jill's eyes were almost level with his nose. She could retreat farther into the woods, but he'd follow—she could tell by the way his gaze seemed to encompass her.

Vince placed his hands on Jill's upper arms, achingly gentle, just as he'd done in her dreams. Her body tensed, poised for flight.

"If you want to end this, Jill, let's end it right." Vince's voice was as tender as his touch. "I want you to be happy, after all."

"I am happy," Jill croaked, her eyes drawn to his

mouth. She wished that things were different, that she had the courage to lean forward and kiss him. Not only was Jill a coward, she had to consider her priorities—Teddy, who wanted to keep Vince, and the fate of Railroad Stop.

Why couldn't she want to kiss someone less complicated, less threatening, less…sexy?

His smile revealed that dimple. "You've been hiding up here, pretending to be happy. Otherwise you would have asked for a divorce a long time ago. You would have fallen in love with someone else."

"Why would you think that?"

"Because I know you."

Jill's body thrummed with electricity generated by Vince's touch. Her heart pounded out a near-frantic cadence for her to escape to. And still she stood paralyzed.

"Tell me about the men you've kissed since we've been married. Whoever's been kissing you has done it all wrong. I'll track them down and beat some sense into each one. I… You're trembling." Vince seemed to notice this last with wonder. His voice softened, lowered. "You need a man in your life who's gentle and patient."

"I haven't kissed anyone," Jill whispered, her eyes still on Vince's mouth, which had drifted closer to hers as he leaned in to catch her words. "I—"

Her response was lost as their lips met.

It didn't matter who closed the gap between them. Vince's lips were soft, his mouth warm against hers. Their contact was awkward as they adjusted for height and comfort, her hesitance and surprise stiffening her spine. And yet Vince was gentle and patient just as he'd promised. On a sigh Jill accepted him, pressing her hands against his shirt, seeking balance as he deepened the kiss.

Why had she waited so long to kiss someone? And not just anyone.

She was kissing her husband!

"I love...the way you kiss," Vince murmured against her mouth, pulling back before breaking this wondrous connection completely. His breath drifted over her skin, into her mouth.

Jill absorbed the moment, absorbed Vince into her shuddering system. Mellow heat spread through her, making her bones feel soft, her body deliciously sinuous. So this was what she'd been missing.

Vince's large hands drifted lazily across Jill's shoulders, skimmed down the slope of her back, creating a tender cocoon around her. She cuddled closer. As if on cue one of Vince's hands slid over the curve of Jill's bottom, the other beneath the hem of her T-shirt. As his hand ventured northward, the warmth of his palm against her spine was electric, sending a startled jolt through Jill's muscles, sending her careering against Vince's hard, powerful chest.

"Oh, baby." Vince hauled her body against him, his kiss no longer gentle, but urgent, demanding, reminiscent of that night Craig hadn't listened when she'd said, *"No!"*

"No!" Jill cried into Vince's mouth, twisting her body and pounding his chest, gasping for air as panic vaulted into her throat. *Not again!*

She fell onto the wet gravel path, sending the air out

of her lungs in a high-pitched whoosh. The clay mountain soil hadn't absorbed the rain from last night. Water soaked through the seat of her jeans. There was little chance of getting into the apartment without Teddy seeing what a mess she was. And she was a mess. She should have known better.

"What the hell?" Vince bent to help Jill up, but she scuttled away, gravel biting into her palms. Vince took a few steps back, his face probably as ashen as hers. "I'm an ass. I should have realized. I'm sorry."

"Don't apologize. Let's just...forget that happened." Would her legs hold her if she stood? She'd been trembling since before they'd kissed. First with anticipation, then with desire and finally with fear.

"We'll go slow next time." Vince extended his hand to Jill once more, his eyes filled with remorse.

"Don't you get it? I can't do this. I haven't since..." Jill scrambled up off the ground before Vince could touch her, giving herself a head rush that nearly sent her tumbling into him. "You got your end-of-the-marriage kiss. I think you should go."

But Vince wasn't listening to her. "Have you talked to someone? A counselor? It's been..."

"I know how long it's been." Sometimes the loneliness was unbearable. When Jill looked at Vince she kept her eyes carefully above his mouth, kept her voice below a freaked-out shriek. "Please leave."

FOR THE SECOND TIME in twenty-four hours, Vince wondered how he'd lost control. The kiss was meant to put Jill in her place, retribution for her asking for a divorce and a way to divert attention from his gut-spilling tirade. The opposite had occurred. It was Vince who had been humbled, Vince who felt sorry.

Vince, the man who had once vowed to protect Jill, had acted nearly as uncontrollably as Craig. It was Jill's panic that sent comprehension surging through Vince's system, quenching his desire as he watched her stumble away from him.

He needed a reality check. This was Jill, with her average curves and her average face. Except...he liked looking at Jill. He always had. Her facial expressions gave away her emotions much too easily, and her smile...he'd always liked her smile. Vince found it hard to believe that she hadn't been smiling at some backwoods sap all this time.

Sure, Jill had a good reason to become celibate eleven years ago—*damn Craig to hell*—but she practically lived like a nun. Vince frowned. Jill had made a home out in the middle of nowhere with a security system Tom Cruise would envy. A man would have to be pretty damn determined if he wanted to infiltrate Jill's defenses. Was it any wonder she hadn't kissed anyone since their wedding day?

Vince stared up at the blue sky, contrasted against the soft green of the pine trees. Jill's personal life was incomplete. Okay, his own personal life wasn't perfect, either, but he was a realist. He'd never be able to hold on to happiness with a woman long-term. It was easier to find a happy medium.

Vince blew out a frustrated breath.

I haven't since...

Jill's words reverberated in his head. She was scared of being with anyone physically. She'd need someone who cared enough to be patient, yet was stubborn enough not to let her hide.

Someone who was staying in her home. Someone obstinate enough not to leave. Someone who'd help reintroduce her to her sexuality and then be gone. Vince smiled. He was the perfect man for no-strings-attached sex.

His smile faded, his gaze drawn again to the sky. Not that he wanted Jill to fall in love with him. And Jill was sentimental enough to read more into this than there was. He'd have to be careful, that was all. His priority was the casino deal, but that didn't mean he couldn't use this unexpected attraction between them to his advantage as he tried to convince Jill that the casino was the right thing for Railroad Stop.

"Vince? Hey, Vince." Teddy came into view on the driveway below. Once he caught sight of Vince, the boy veered with coltish steps onto the gravel path. As he got nearer, Vince could see his mouth drawn in a sad pout. "I wanted to say goodbye."

"Are you going somewhere, buddy?"

"Not me, *you*. Mom said you were leaving." Squinting against the sun only made Teddy look sadder.

"I'm not going anywhere."

"But Mom said—"

"Edda Mae said I could have a shower first."

"I don't know. Mom said—"

"Why don't you let me worry about your mom?"

Teddy tilted his head to one side and scrunched up his nose. "Are you sure you want to do that?"

"I'll talk to her." Vince bent down to Teddy's level, ready to put his plan into action. "In the meantime…"

"WHAT DO YOU MEAN you're not leaving?" Jill propped her hands on her hips and glared at Vince. She stood in the crook of the kitchen, about as far away from Vince's position on the couch as she could get without leaving the apartment.

Vince's kiss had been incredibly magnetic, making her want more, and earth-shatteringly scary, making her...confused. Jill didn't do more. She didn't do kisses. Just thinking about kissing had left Jill hot and cold for years, wondering if she could go further, if she could make love with someone.

Well, this proved it. Jill couldn't. Vince had to go. Only he didn't seem to want to take the hammer-over-the-head hint that Jill wanted him to leave.

"I've decided it's more convenient to stay. Here." Vince pointed at the living room carpet, but Jill could just as easily picture him rubbing his hands in glee because now he was going to be around to mess with her head.

"You can't stay." Jill paced the limits of the tiny kitchen because Vince was in the living room, and after what had happened earlier, distance was called for. Vince's impact on Jill was unexpected. One minute Jill wanted to comfort him, the next bop him over the head, and then she found herself wanting to fall into his arms.

"You'd throw me out? I'm your husband."

Jill's mouth fell open, but she quickly recovered. "Soon to be divorced, remember?"

"Jill. Be reasonable. What will people think if I don't stay here?"

"The same thing they've been thinking for ten

years." She pinned Vince with her gaze. "My husband is either a loser or he's dead."

Vince's eyebrows shot up. "You told them I was dead?"

"No." She hadn't told them Vince was a loser, either.

"I'll make it worth your while." There was a smile lurking behind those seemingly innocent, dark eyes of his as he sprawled in the corner of her couch and watched her.

He wouldn't proposition her, would he? Jill's heart pounded faster.

Vince opened his mouth to speak.

"Choose your terms carefully," Jill warned. If he so much as breathed inappropriately, he was out of there.

Vince's dimple flashed. "I'm offering you free labor. But if you want me to pay to stay here, that's fine, too. You can't send me away. It's obvious we need time to settle our personal business."

"Obvious to you, maybe. We agreed to divorce." By supreme willpower, Jill refrained from spinning her wedding ring. Once Vince left this morning, she could post her signs and begin planning a campaign against him and his casino.

"I didn't agree to a divorce." Vince stood. He'd showered and now looked every inch the corporate citizen in his fine wool slacks, white shirt and tie. "How about I toss in something even better? I'll include you in my meetings pertaining to the casino."

"Why would you do that?" It gave Jill a huge advantage over Vince and Arnie.

Vince pinned Jill with his gaze. "With an inside look you'll come to see a casino as the best thing for this town and to Shady Oak. You could offer weekend gambling getaways. This way you'll have plenty of opportunity to talk with Arnie privately."

How dare he? Jill tried to laugh but it came out more like a squeak.

"Afraid?" Vince challenged, still staring at her.

"I wanted you gone. I'll let you stay, but only for another day, two max," she added when Vince smiled too quickly.

"He's staying?" Teddy rushed across the room at Jill's nod and hugged her. He must have been eavesdropping in the hallway. "And I didn't even have to promise to be good. Thank you."

"Yes, thank you," Vince echoed, flashing Jill his trust-me smile minus the dimple. He winked at Teddy. "You won't regret it."

Jill already did. She remembered falling under Vince's spell, bending to his arguments about the marriage. Vince was bound to captivate the town just as easily. And she'd invited him to stay here? She had to be nuts.

"Don't you have any other clothes besides a suit?" Jill snapped shrewishly before shaking her head at Vince. "Oh, never mind. Meet me out at the garage."

Vince obediently left the apartment, most unusual for a man who argued with her about everything. Teddy put on rubber cleaning gloves and picked up the caddy without a word of protest, most unusual for a boy who normally dragged his feet when it came to chores. Was Teddy that excited about Vince staying?

Teddy blinked, his grin never fading. "Have you seen my goggles?"

Jill reached past Teddy beneath the sink for a pair of ski goggles. Teddy liked to pretend he was a mad scientist when he cleaned. Actually, he liked to pretend he cleaned. Mostly he kept Jill and Edda Mae company. Jill eased the goggles over his thin face.

"Thanks, Mom." His eyes were masked behind orange plastic. "Gotta go help Edda Mae."

"Everything okay?" Vince asked when Jill joined him a few minutes later. His damp hair gleamed blue-black in the morning sun.

"Do I look like...? Oh, never mind." Jill sighed. What was done was done. At least now she knew to keep her guard up. "Could you load these signs into Edda Mae's truck?"

"The NO CASINO signs?" he asked. "Why, exactly, am I helping you with these? I can clean rooms." Vince pointed to Teddy and Edda Mae disappearing into a guest bungalow.

"Since you refuse to leave, I get to choose how you earn your keep."

Vince gestured to their previous night's work. "But these are—"

"Signs against you." Jill cut him off with a smug smile. That was what he got for trying to intimidate her with a kiss.

"I said I was sorry," Vince said, reading her mind. He tucked his tie in between two buttons midplacket.

"Don't apologize." If only she'd had some warning. If only she'd realized what Vince had in mind....

Jill jerked back a step. "I didn't want you to kiss me." It was vital Vince know she hadn't led him on.

"Really." With a dimpled smile Vince looked down

at Jill. If he could read her thoughts, they were probably just as confusing to him as they were to her. But he kept on smiling as if something she'd done amused him. Maybe it was the way Jill kissed. Or maybe she had a smudge of dirt on her nose. Whatever it was, Vince wasn't taking her declaration seriously.

Jill pointed at the signs, frustration emanating from every pore. "I need these signs loaded in the truck—*now*—so I can post them and people will know Railroad Stop opposes outside moneymen."

Vince tried to argue but Jill stalked away, returning periodically with stakes for the signs, piling them into the back of Edda Mae's dented old white pickup alongside the stacks of signs Vince had made. Jill also stowed a nail gun and a shovel from the garage. When they were finished loading, she latched the tailgate, called a cheery goodbye to Vince and climbed behind the driver's seat. She grinned. She was free of him.

The passenger door creaked open as Vince hopped in beside Jill.

"You're not coming with me."

"You wanted my help." A smile played at the corners of his mouth.

"You're done helping me." Jill fiddled with the truck key.

"And put you behind schedule? Not a chance." Vince fastened the seat belt. "How long will it take you to dig the holes, post the signs and make sure they're stable?"

"Most of the day."

"I don't have most of the day and neither do you. Let's go." Vince reached across Jill's lap to snag the key, sliding it into the ignition. The truck sputtered to life. He kept his fingers on the key. She could feel his eyes on her as palpably as a caress.

Jill didn't move. In fact, Jill wasn't sure she was breathing. If she turned her head it wouldn't take much to close the distance between them, to feel his warm body pressed to hers. Married couples kissed all the time. But Vince wasn't her husband, fantasy or otherwise, not really. He wanted to gut Railroad Stop.

"Stop it." Jill thrust his hand away. "You don't… These signs…"

"Are important to you."

She did look at Vince then, allowing herself to stare into eyes so dark brown they were almost black. Yet there was no mockery there, no sarcasm.

"Friends—" Vince stressed the word "—help friends. I made a promise on our wedding day. I'll always be there for you, Jill."

"Whether I like it or not. Why, Vince? Why?" With a slight shake of her head, Jill answered her own question, suspecting Vince was directing her down a path where she'd have to make a choice. "Till death—" or divorce "—do us part."

CHAPTER SEVEN

"WHY HAVEN'T I HEARD from Vince?" Aldo called to his secretary the moment he came in the door of his personal quarters at the Sicilian Saturday morning. "He doesn't answer his phone. Where's my e-mail? Why don't you know why I haven't heard from him?"

"Mr. Patrizio, did you call me down here on a Saturday because you've forgotten how to retrieve your messages?" Ernie paused on the gold-and-white marble entry in front of a tile mosaic of the waterways of Venice. After years as a semiprofessional gambler, Ernie had come to work for Aldo last spring. He was the first secretary—correction, personal assistant, as Ernie preferred to be called—with any backbone. It was a rare day he didn't talk back at his boss.

Who would have thought Ernie had such gumption?

"I haven't forgotten. You don't program the things properly," Aldo grumbled, pushing his worthless BlackBerry across his desk. It wasn't his responsibility to figure out all the buttons on the gadgets he owned. It was Ernie's.

Instead of storming off, Ernie set his briefcase on the foyer table with a solid thump. "They're programmed perfectly."

"Ha! Then why don't I have any messages?"

"If you don't want to learn how to use technology, why do you buy all this stuff?" Ernie crossed the room on sturdy legs. He was short and solid in both physical appearance and temperament, but he had no fashion sense. Today he wore an Elvis bowling shirt, black shorts and leather hippy sandals. Not exactly appropriate office attire.

Rosalie would have liked Ernie. Aldo hid a smile behind his scowl. "Because a man of my position must have those things." Or he'd be thought weak by those young MBAs.

"Maybe no one wants to talk to you. Have you thought of that? You're as bad as Maddy used to be, throwing tantrums at the drop of a hat."

Guilt reared its ugly head. Aldo had forgotten Ernie watched six year-old Maddy on Saturdays as partial payment for his room and board. "I'm Italian. That's what we do." But his retort lacked his usual sting. He stood and moved aside to let Ernie work his magic at the desk, receiving a whiff of the after-shave Ernie insisted on drenching himself with.

"How's your wife today?" Ernie asked.

"Fine. She'll likely wake up tomorrow." Despite more than eighteen months in a coma, Aldo still maintained to others that Rosalie would come back to him. There had been several episodes in the past year where she'd stopped breathing, as if she'd finally given up. But Aldo wouldn't let her. He loved her too much.

"We can only hope she does. Heaven knows I could use someone else to keep you in line." Ernie started with Aldo's BlackBerry, then did something with his cell phone and finally clicked whatever mysterious buttons were needed to open the e-mail program on the computer. "You don't have any messages."

"Are you sure? Vince had that meeting last night."

"On a Friday? I know where he gets his work ethic," Ernie quipped.

"I want a status report."

"And I want two days a week off."

"When I started this business I worked—"

"Seven days a week for ten years." Ernie moved the mouse contraption around on the desk and then started typing. "It probably snowed while you were building this high-rise, too."

"I don't know why I haven't fired you."

"I don't know why you haven't given me a raise."

Aldo snorted. "Maybe if you found my messages, I would."

"The best I can do is send one to Vince. See?" Ernie pointed to the screen. "'Update me on Indian casino ASAP.' Good enough?"

"It'll do." Unlike Aldo's last few secretaries, Ernie didn't sugarcoat his communications with niceties, even ones sent to Vince. Although Aldo would have liked to at least mention that Rosalie's condition was the same, he didn't want to keep Ernie from his Saturday activities any longer than he had already.

Besides, the point in sending Vince away was to make him into a man, the kind who could run the Sicilian, putting it above everything else in his life. Aldo wouldn't coddle the boy and tell him he missed him. He shared Vince's disappointment with every deal that slipped through his fingers, but it wasn't Aldo's way to commiserate. Vince was too old to be pampered.

VINCE WAS on edge.

"Your shoes are ruined," Jill pointed out in her unrelenting quest to piss Vince off.

She was right. Last night's rain had left the air fresh and the ground soft muck. Standing in eight inches of wet grass on a steep, sunny slope, Vince's loafers were caked in mud, his socks no better off, his feet cold. He wanted to wrap Jill in his arms and kiss her until her warmth made his toes curl. But he also wanted to tell her to give it a rest—not exactly in those words. And so he clenched his teeth and followed her lead by avoiding talking about the casino.

"My shoes are no more ruined than they were last night when you splashed paint on them." When she'd first used him.

"Yeah, but now your pants are trashed, too," she said.

"Right." His trousers dragged with inches of soggy, dirty cuff. Vince was starting to question his judgment in helping Jill with her signs. He should have insisted he work with Teddy, even if it meant donning a pair of ski goggles and gloves. Instead, he'd chosen Chinese water torture—this slow ping-ping on his nerves until he wanted to scream in frustration. That was Jill. His wife.

Jill held a sign propped on its posts waiting for him to finish his hole. With her auburn hair held in that loose, curly ponytail Jill was nothing like the adorably awkward debutante of her youth, but probably looked a damn sight better than Vince did. She stood just out of reach, her faded jeans tucked into rubber boots, her shirt buttoned but untucked. A man needed a good imagination to identify Jill's curves beneath all that baggy flannel. Good thing Vince could supplement the gaps with the memory of her body flattened against his.

During their first few stops, Jill kept busy attaching the thin posts to the signs with a nail gun while Vince made holes in the claylike earth. This was a workout in itself and not conducive to conversation. Now that all the signs were done, Jill stood by watching Vince dig and trying to pick apart his self-control.

"I've never seen a man dig a hole with a tie on," Jill said. "Or cufflinks."

"You know me. It's all about the clothes." If Jill believed that, she didn't know him at all.

"No. With you it was all about the cars. Fast, sleek, sexy." Jill thrust out her chin, unaware that he wanted to kiss that mutinous expression off her face if only to shut her up. "You liked your women that way, too. Which is why—"

"I'd prefer we talk about the present, not the past." Vince stared at the reddish-brown mud tumbling from the edge of the hole onto the shovel, wishing she hadn't recalled that aspect of his youth. "I know you don't want a casino here, Jill, but I'm going to build one. My grandfather—"

"Need any help?" An elderly woman with silver Princess Leia braids slowed her faded blue, late-model SUV. She leaned over and looked at the odd pair on the side of the road. Her tire rims were so rusty Vince was surprised they didn't shatter into pieces, leaving the vehicle sitting on its axles.

Vince recognized the older woman from the meeting

the night before. Great. He looked like a grave digger instead of a man with millions of dollars at his disposal.

"We're fine, Mildred," Jill assured her. "Just putting up a few signs. I can count on your support, can't I?"

Mildred hesitated and Vince could feel her curiosity burning, could feel an opportunity slipping away. To hell with looking like a grave digger. Vince quit battling the sodden earth and turned, wobbling as his foot began to slip over the edge of the hole. Lurching with the shovel, he dragged it back up the side, filling the space between his shoe and his arch with cold mud, but his smile never wavered.

Jill steadied him, her grip surprisingly strong and reassuring, a direct contrast to her laughter.

Jill was laughing at him?

Vince shook her off, trying to unclench his teeth. "Where do you stand on the casino issue, Mildred?"

"Why I...I haven't decided yet." One of her pale, thin hands fluttered in the air as her SUV idled roughly. "Just look at it. It's a lovely piece of property. And yet, it could do such good for everyone."

"Not everyone," Jill muttered.

"That's okay. Jill's made up her mind, but I think everyone's entitled to their own opinion, don't you, Mildred? Let me know if you want to talk about it. I'm staying with Jill at Shady Oak." He waved dismissively, anger bubbling as he realized he was standing on the property being considered for the casino. They criss-crossed the valley so much he'd lost his sense of direction. The sooner Mildred left, the sooner Vince could strangle Jill.

Mildred's brow furrowed and she said something

Vince didn't catch before she drove off at a leisurely pace that would have gotten her run off the road in Vegas. Her SUV backfired as it coughed and stammered its way up the next hill.

"Were you ever going to tell me this is the property?" Vince sought firmer purchase as he spun unsteadily on Jill.

"Nope." She smirked.

Vince took the sign from Jill and stuck it in the ground, holding it steady while Jill pounded the stakes with an intensity that betrayed her annoyance. Vince kept quiet, clamping down on the anger, the frustration, the ever-present desire Jill elicited since they'd kissed. To distract himself, he concentrated on a strategy for Railroad Stop's mayor, whom he wanted to speak with later. Hopefully he'd be able to address the mayor's specific concerns about the casino.

"You're just trying to win Mildred's vote." Jill swung the hammer with stronger-than-necessary strokes, as if she was imagining pounding Vince's head.

He drew a deep breath. He had to walk a fine line. There was so much more at play here than a financial deal. "I want a chance to tell my side, unlike you, who just wants to tell Mildred what to think."

Jill set her lips in a thin line, which was just as frustrating as a verbal denial.

Vince chose his next words carefully as he filled in the hole. "A casino is an investment in the future when the alternative is a town that might cease to exist because people have to move somewhere else to make a living. If everybody stopped to look at the issues, they'd see that vacation homes are seasonal, but a casino draws a crowd year-round."

Jill made a derogatory sound that ran like a tremor beneath his skin. "You are so full of it. You don't care what this does to anyone, do you?" Better than any drill sergeant, she'd pushed and pushed until anger rolled over Vince in an unstoppable rush, flattening reason and rational thought.

"You're so quick to judge," he said, "but you haven't really given the idea of a casino a chance. Just like you didn't give me a chance in Vegas. Maybe if you'd listen to me now you'd be able to find Teddy a father. There are lots of men out there who'd find you attractive." So much for willpower and patience.

And *snap*—Jill's bluster was gone, replaced by rapid-fire emotions—naive surprise in her widened eyes, heart-wrenching wariness as she drew back, then reluctant regret in the set of her lips.

"Stop it." Jill retreated down the slippery slope to Edda Mae's truck. When her boots met the pavement, she wheeled about, so full of indignation that she stamped her feet, sending reddish-brown mud clods flying. "How could anyone have anything real with *me?*" Jill's voice cracked and then she closed her eyes as if the admission hurt.

It must be painful to carry such a belief. It wasn't just Vince's toes that were cold now. His veins had turned to ice. Jill thought she was less of a woman because of what Craig did to her. All these years later, Vince wished he'd tried harder to convince Jill to go with him on Senior Ditch night. But he'd been the class misfit, not the golden boy, just as helpless to protect Jill as he'd been to protect himself from his own family trials.

Vince's fingers twitched on the shovel. This sleepy town was Jill's crutch. She'd gated her house and she was going to control growth in town by gating that, too. Which would hold her back even more.

Jill stood, a bundle of insecurity, her arms wrapped tightly about her chest, eyes cast down and blinking back tears. Vince was bringing in a casino that, in her mind, would have a revolving door of men who didn't live here, who'd shatter her composure.

Vince swore. He was closer than he'd ever been to closing a deal. There wasn't time to broker another one. His grandfather's offer to bankroll a project would evaporate come November first. If it came down to himself or Jill, he'd have to choose himself.

And then Jill wiped away a tear.

Without knowing what he had in mind, Vince suddenly morphed into a bundle of energy. Unfortunately he had less practice descending mountainous slopes than Jill, particularly in thick, suction-cup-like mud. He skidded several feet, nearly pitched face-forward when his shoes became entrenched in the muck, righted himself by using the shovel and then leaped the last yard to the road, catching himself against Edda Mae's white front fender with a bone-denting crunch that was going to hurt much more tomorrow.

Vince spun on Jill, opening his mouth to speak, although he still didn't know what he was going to say. He only knew it had to be something to comfort her.

"Are you okay? You're a mess," Jill said.

"I'm a mess?" Vince mumbled, bending down to

catch his reflection in the side mirror. His hair was spiked by the wind, dirt smudged one cheek and his shirt was speckled with mud. His pants sagged halfway down his hips from the weight of mud and water. If his dad saw him...

Vince stiffened. If his dad saw him looking like this, he'd have beat the crap out of him. "We're leaving. Get in the truck."

All of Vince's maddening corporate composure was gone, replaced by a vulnerability that surprised her. Jill tried to remember what might have caused such a change in Vince, but she'd been too upset by his remarks to pay attention to what she'd been saying. "What? Are you afraid that people will see us together and pity you for marrying me in the first place?"

Before Jill registered what was happening, Vince had her backed against the rust-spotted truck bed, his face so close she could feel his hot breath on her cheek, could remember how hard it would be to breathe when he covered her mouth with his large hand and told her this was what she wanted.

Vince gritted his teeth and practically snarled at her. "Damn it. What's wrong with you? Don't *ever* let me hear you talk about yourself like that again. Don't give him that power over you. Don't give *anyone* that power over you." Then Vince's eyes seemed to grow distant, as if seeing something dark in his own past, and he drew back infinitesimally.

The combination of Vince's protectiveness and that glimpse into his own torment gave Jill the strength to move, to realize that Vince wouldn't hurt her. She'd superimposed memories of Craig onto Vince, and

Vince wasn't like that. He'd cared for her once. Jill patted Vince on the arm with a trembling hand and edged away.

Vince glanced down at where she'd touched him, still visibly shaken. "Is the only reason you don't want a casino here because there'll be too many strangers— too many men—around town?"

Exposed, Jill moved to the rear of the truck. "If your casino goes through, my guests will step out on my porch and see your generators, air-conditioning units and a parking garage. How could anyone retreat from the world with a view like that?" Jill was at a disadvantage. She didn't know why he'd come here. "If you chose Railroad Stop because of me, because you thought I'd benefit, think again."

"You had nothing to do with me coming here." Vince set the muddy shovel in the truck, eyebrows furrowed.

Unexpected disappointment slipped past her defenses. Jill walked around to the driver's side. "I can just as easily start somewhere else." What a lie. Starting over would be torture, not to mention financially impossible.

"That didn't come out right. I knew you were here and when Arnie's inquiry reached me, it just clicked," Vince explained, seeming to notice he'd upset her. He leaned his forearms on the truck bed and gave Jill a lopsided smile. "Before we go any further I need you to know why—"

"I don't need to know anything."

"Yes, you do. This project is important to me. And not because of the money," Vince added quickly, then sighed. "I have been, and always will be, a screwup."

"You're wrong," Jill blurted. Vince certainly had all the trappings of success. And he'd always seemed so confident.

Smiling sadly, Vince wiped his mud-streaked cheek a few times on his shoulder as if it itched. "After my grandmother's accident, the police couldn't find the driver who hit her. I became...obsessed with identifying who had left her in a coma." He shrugged. "After a while I was convinced my grandfather had arranged the *accident.*"

"You know he didn't." She could tell by Vince's expression. "He wouldn't. He loves her too much." Even Jill, who barely knew his grandparents, had seen Aldo Patrizio's love for his wife in a touch, a smile, a glance.

"I know that now. My friend Sam told me repeatedly that I was wrong, but I couldn't accept it. And my grandfather—jeez—he had no patience for me anymore, probably because he was so worried about my grandmother. After I did something particularly stupid, he offered to finance me in my own venture on the condition that I seal the deal within a year." Vince stared at his dirty hands. "If I fail, he's done with me. No job. No inheritance. Nothing. That was last October. And here I am in mid-September, empty-handed."

Vince wasn't empty-handed. He had Arnie in his pocket. Jill was fooling herself if she believed her signs could stop this. Just listening to Vince's story almost made her want to pull for him. And his arguments for the projects made sense, just not for her.

"Railroad Stop is ideal. The atmosphere, the land available, the prep work that's already been done. Everything is lining up on this one." Vince laughed once, mirthlessly. "Almost everything."

"So what? You can move on." Easier than she could. "You can make this work and generate even more money in a bigger town." Jill grimaced at her calculated response. She had never been able to shake her parents' pragmatism.

"This isn't about the money."

"Really." Having grown up in Vegas, Jill wasn't buying it. "Your grandfather could have sent you on a scavenger hunt to prove yourself, but he didn't. He sent you out to make a deal."

"I know it's a test. If our positions were reversed, I'd probably need some kind of proof, too." Vince shifted his arms and stared at the shovel. "We're alike in many ways, but not in one respect. Everything he touches turns to gold. Everything I try falls apart. I'm a failure."

"You're not a failure." Jill pounded her fist on the truck bed when she would have liked to pound his head. "You graduated from high school. You graduated from college. You…served in the army. You must have done something right. You came home alive." So many young men weren't as fortunate. "You drive a new Porsche, for crying out loud." The last new car Jill owned had been given to her by her parents. Every spare nickel had gone into her savings and now into Shady Oak.

Vince picked at a rusty flake of paint on the truck for what seemed like a long time before answering. "None of that matters now. If I don't prove to my grandfather that I can make things happen on my own, he'll push me away. And then he'll be all alone in his penthouse with my grandmother."

As much as this tugged at Jill's heart, she had to protect herself and Teddy and stand firm against Vince's project. "If you're telling me you won't back off from the casino, I can accept that, even respect you for it, given the pressure you're under. But I'm still opposed to it."

Wearing a wicked smile that promised too much, Vince shook his head. "You can't be that heartless. I'm going to lose everything."

Jill gasped. "Like I won't? You are such a jerk. Did you really think that story would make me support your casino?"

"It's not a story." But Vince was still smiling as he shrugged. "Hey, you can't fault a guy for trying."

A truck crested the hill down the road.

Looking at his clothes, Vince said, "I need to clean up. Let's head back."

"Not yet. I've got to put this last sign up in town." She'd like to put it somewhere else.

"No." Vince's voice was firm. "No. I'm not going into town like this."

"You can sit in the truck and wait." Jill hauled open the driver's door, convinced this was just more of his failure malarkey.

With a sigh, Vince climbed into the truck, his shoes hitting the floorboards with a noticeable *squish,* mud clumps falling from both sides of his feet. "When did you become so evil?"

Even though Jill knew Vince was joking, it hurt.

You wanted it just as bad as I did. Admit it. You couldn't have kissed me like that and not known what we were going to do.

Craig was right. She'd sent out the wrong message. Maybe deep down Jill had wanted to be something more than the boring debutante with good grades. "How do you know I haven't always been evil?"

"Hey. It was a joke." Vince touched her shoulder. When Jill didn't speak, he added, "People say things they don't mean all the time. You've got to be one of the kindest, least evil people I know…your present manipulation of me regarding *those* signs excepted."

"If I'm such a good person, why did such a terrible thing happen to me?" Jill immediately wanted to snatch back the words that had haunted her for so long. She'd never said as much to Edda Mae. Why was she whining to Vince? Especially when he'd just tried to hoodwink her?

"Pull over."

Biting, Jill kept driving.

"Pull over. Now." The menace in Vince's tone left no room for argument.

Jill did as he asked, then sat gripping the wheel, staring ahead and gluing her lips together.

"Are you going to explain that last comment to me or make me tickle it out of you?" Vince made a half-hearted attempt to poke her in the ribs.

Jill shook her head, swatting away his hand. "Don't joke about it."

"Whatever Craig said to you to make you feel so small is all bullshit," Vince said quietly. "Even my dad, who was a crappy father on the best of days, told me more than once that when a woman says no, it means stop. If you've been thinking all this time that what happened was your fault, you're crazy."

"But I kissed him. I let him…" This was mortifying. *"I let him touch me."*

"That doesn't matter." Vince pried Jill's fingers from the steering wheel. He held onto her hand as if it was the most fragile thing he'd ever touched. "He was wrong. No means no means no. Making love is a one hundred percent agreement. Going all the way means the woman wants to go all the way, up to and including the last part of the way."

His words drained her. Jill risked what little pride she had left and glanced at him. Vince looked as if he'd been run over by a truck with his dirt-smudged face, mussed hair and far-too-serious expression. She tried to lighten the moment with a wobbly smile. "I know we're married and all, but that was too heavy, especially when you just tried to play me."

Vince didn't smile back. "Shh. Give it a while. Crap takes a long time to get over."

Jill nodded, touched that Vince knew exactly what she needed to hear, yet still embarrassed beyond belief.

And then Vince tucked a strand of hair behind Jill's ear, leaving a distracting trail of heat.

Jill wanted to kiss him. Or was it her fantasy Vince? The lines between them were blurring. "I can't even kiss anyone. My head just goes back to that night and I know it could happen again. It's better if I don't lead anyone on. Ever."

Vince sat up straight. "Wait a minute. You blame yourself for me kissing you?"

"Yes, I—"

"I practically chased you into the woods," Vince pointed out.

Jill frowned. But she hadn't run away.

"I chased you," he said again. "And the way you were kissing me had me wanting to back you against a tree." Vince took her chin in his hand and forced her to face him, to stare into his deep, serious eyes. "But you said no."

"I said no to Craig, too."

"When a guy really cares about you, he'll wait, years if he has to."

Jill made a disparaging noise. As if Vince had waited for her all this time. "You came here to punish me, didn't you?" As if what she'd been through wasn't punishment enough. "I may have accepted the longest pity date on the planet from you, but you don't have to string me along and pretend to like me."

When he offered no defense, Jill pulled out onto the road, gunning the truck over a rise past the rickety gas station on the edge of town and down Railroad Stop's Main Street. She drove past the smattering of faded, older-model trucks and sedans facing outside the porch-lined storefronts. It was like traveling through a time warp. Her clients loved visiting the quaint little shops along Main Street. Jill could appreciate its charm, but that didn't erase the facts—she wasn't really married, Vince didn't love her. All she could do was stop, stand up for what she believed in and hope she could keep Vince from changing this place.

"Should you be parking here?" Vince asked as Jill waited for a lone car to pass before she turned into her spot. "The sign says that's the mayor's parking space."

"It is." Jill hopped out the door, letting a rare glimpse of pride show on her face. "I'm the mayor."

CHAPTER EIGHT

WHY THE HELL hadn't Arnie come right out and told Vince his wife was the mayor?

And why the hell hadn't Jill told Vince she was the mayor?

Dragging inches of soggy trouser, Vince stomped after Jill as she crossed the raised wooden sidewalk lugging her last purple, green and red sign. With wet, muddy leather on his feet and muck-sodden wool up to his knees, Vince clenched his jaw to keep from shouting at Jill as she unlocked the glass door with *Mayor* stenciled in gold letters.

As Jill swung the door open, a bell tinkled loudly enough to be heard three stores down, announcing the arrival of a fool.

"You must think I'm an idiot," he said. Contrary to their roadside conversation, Jill wasn't a helpless woman in need of rescuing. Nobody elected that kind of person into office. Vince kept thinking he understood his wife when it was becoming clearer that he knew nothing about her or how to talk her around to the casino.

"You're the mayor." Vince jabbed his finger at Jill.

He disregarded the vibration at his hip, announcing his BlackBerry had finally received a strong-enough signal to download his messages.

"Yes." Ignoring him, Jill yanked on the cord to raise the dusty aluminum blinds on the front window.

Vince stabbed his finger in her direction again. "You don't want the casino."

Jill gave him a crooked smile that showed not an ounce of remorse, making him want to kiss that smug look right off her face. "That's correct." Then Jill propped the NO CASINO sign on the window ledge and lowered the blinds behind it.

Vince sank into an old, wood-and-red leather captain's chair. She *was* evil.

Sure, Jill was only trying to defend her turf. That didn't keep Vince from coming to a slow boil as he remembered painting the signs with her last night and recalled the look on Jill's face just now when she told him she was the mayor. She was sending out signals only the class idiot wouldn't pick up on—that the priorities in her life were herself and Teddy. No one else mattered.

"You betrayed me," Vince whispered, rubbing his chest absently.

And still Vince was aware of his need to bury his face in her silky hair, wanted to taste her lips again. He'd been working too hard, had neglected his personal life too long. His gaze drifted to the window. There had to be other attractive women in Railroad Stop. Except the entire town knew he was married to Jill.

"Can you say you haven't betrayed me in some

way, too?" Jill couldn't seem to look at him when she asked the question.

At once Vince knew Jill wasn't talking about the casino. She was referring to their wedding vows. Vince had never offered his heart to another, but that didn't mean he lived like a monk. Lots of women visiting Vegas were looking for a man like Vince, a man who enjoyed a bit of fun but wasn't interested in anything more than a night or two of meaningless sex. But Jill had honored their vows even though she'd left him. If this was a real marriage, Vince would be on his knees, groveling for her forgiveness.

"I'm sorry," Vince mumbled, surprising himself. It didn't matter that he hadn't been with a woman in over a year. The hurt in Jill's eyes was humbling.

The phone rang. It was an antique, cream-colored, with a circular dial and an authentic ring. In fact, the entire office was out of *Mayberry R.F.D.*—old, warped aerial photographs of the valley hung on one wall, while pictures of past mayors lined the wall behind a dented metal desk that sat on scuffed black-and-white-checked linoleum. Only the computer looked as if it came from this century.

"Hello, Arnie," Jill answered, avoiding Vince's eyes. "Yes, he's here with me. I showed him the property under consideration. He got out and got his feet wet." Jill gave Vince's wrecked shoes a significant glance, her mouth curling up on one side. "Will do."

She hung up. "Arnie saw us drive by. He wants to see you."

Vince gazed down at his clothes, struck by a memory of his father tossing him against the wall when he'd been unable to knot his tie properly. He must have been six or seven, his mother too drunk on the couch to protest. His father took any sign of imperfection as an excuse to punish Vince.

It was important to coddle Arnie, Vince's biggest supporter, but also to present himself as a dignified, capable leader. It would take twenty minutes to drive to Jill's, ten minutes or so to clean up and change and another twenty to get back.

"Arnie can wait."

"Arnie's not used to waiting," Jill said, forehead wrinkling as if she, too, knew he should be sucking up to the tribal leader.

"I can't go anywhere like this," he said, hating that he sounded like a pouting prima donna.

She laughed, giving him the once-over. "Appearances don't mean—"

"Appearances are everything and you know it, but obviously you've forgotten." Annoyance drove Vince to his feet. If he showed up looking like this, Arnie would realize Vince couldn't handle his business. Arnie would be backpedaling instantly.

Mechanically, Vince opened the door, barely hearing the jangle of the bell above him. From his search to find the meeting yesterday, he had a basic understanding of the layout of Main Street and knew where Arnie's business was. He should just go and let things fall apart naturally. It would be one more checkmark on his long list of failures.

Vince opened his mouth to command Jill to come along, but then he saw his reflection in the glass.

SO MUCH FOR VINCE promising to include Jill in all his meetings.

Thirty-five minutes after Vince left, Jill had dusted the place, created some flyers informing residents of the importance of the issues being discussed at the city council meeting the following week, stuck them on windshields up and down Main Street, and finished reading an e-mail sent by a neighboring town's mayor expressing his support for a casino in Railroad Stop.

Sure. As long as it isn't in his backyard.

Vince and Arnie were probably finalizing the deal while she posted a date and time for the next meeting in the office window. Any moment she expected a phone call from Arnie announcing the need for a special town vote.

Maybe Jill should have told Vince that she was the mayor, but during most of their arguments she'd been too flustered by his presence and his effect on her to work it into the conversation. Besides, being mayor of Railroad Stop was more of a figurehead position than a legislative one. Her most important job was coordinating elections and special voting events, like the bond measure they'd need to pass to build the roads, sewers and electrical systems needed for the new housing development.

The tinkle of the antique bell over the mayor's door announced a visitor. Jill glanced up, ready to flash a smile of welcome, and then froze.

"Let's go." Vince wore crisp new jeans, boots and a white, long-sleeved Western shirt with a blue-checked yoke and pearly buttons. He looked like any other able-bodied male from the California foothills ready to pick a fight or break a heart after a long workweek. He dropped a bulky plastic bag by the door.

"Did Arnie give you clean clothes?"

Vince scowled. "I haven't been to Arnie's yet. I went to the feed store for these. Come on."

"Arnie didn't invite me." People in Railroad Stop didn't leave Arnie cooling his jets or show up when he didn't want them. Jill tried to hang on to a smile. Arnie had wanted to buy Shady Oak. When he learned that Edda Mae had sold it to Jill, Arnie had suddenly found Jill interesting. It was almost as if he didn't believe she had a husband. What a surprise for him.

"I don't care." Vince swung the door open. "Move your butt."

"I...uh..." She'd admit it to herself. Arnie intimidated her. Add Vince to the equation and this wasn't going to be pleasant for Jill.

"You're the mayor, right?" There was an edge to Vince's tone that Jill didn't understand.

"Ye-es."

"You need to keep your eye on the opposition, right?" Vince tapped his chest.

"Yes." Jill drew the word out suspiciously.

"Then show some backbone." Vince held the door open wider.

"It's not a lack of backbone." Jill grabbed her keys. "It's more like United Nations peacekeeping guidelines. Arnie plays in his sandbox and I play in mine. But if you want me to go with you, I will."

After Jill locked up they walked toward Arnie's place, booted feet echoing on the wood sidewalk and announcing their approach. In Railroad Stop that meant everyone would come running to check who was passing by and see the mayor with her devastatingly handsome husband.

"The buildings on both sides of this block were built over one hundred years ago," Jill said. "It's the heart of the original town."

Vince paused to poke a toe at a rotted board next to a large wine-barrel planter filled with pink blossoms. "Is it the original wood, too?"

"No, but regardless of which plan goes through, we will be giving downtown a serious makeover."

Joe Mattwell, the town's burly baker, appeared at the doorway of his store wearing a full-length stained apron. "Hey, Jill. Is this the man behind the casino?"

Despite a strong compulsion to yank Vince away so that he wouldn't swing Joe to his cause, Jill introduced the two men and then listened impatiently as they talked.

"I'd love to hear what you have to say when you have more time," Joe said before disappearing back into the bakery.

"He seems to want the deal to go through," Vince noted.

"Just because he wants to hear you speak doesn't mean he's interested in a casino. He was just being polite. Everyone's curious about you and willing to do anything for a tidbit of gossip. People up here think I'm married."

"You *are* married," he reminded her darkly. "To me."

For how much longer? Jill spun her wedding ring with one thumb as they passed several empty storefronts. She knew she couldn't have it both ways, but she liked her life as it was.

Bang-bang! Thunk.

Jill was slammed against the wall with a large back

in front of her face. "Ow." She'd hit her head against the wall and it hurt. "Vince, move." She could barely breathe, and when she did the smell of new clothing filled her nostrils. "Vince!" She shoved him away.

He turned around and looked at her dazedly, then scanned the area. He'd said he'd served in the war and there had certainly been enough news coverage on post-traumatic stress.

"Vince." Jill tugged him around to look at her. "A car backfired."

"A car?" Vince was recovering quickly. He blinked and seemed his normal self once more.

Mark Oberle, the local grocer, walked to the edge of the sidewalk across the street and waved. "Jill! Wait a minute." He crossed the road for an introduction.

Biting her lip, Jill was able to hang on to her composure while the two men talked about the business opportunities a casino would bring. What she would have liked to have done was grill Vince on his reaction to the car. He'd had a similar episode when Edda Mae dropped the frying pan this morning. Did he have any other problems? Was he expected to get over them on his own?

"I haven't made up my mind yet. This town is ready to grow," Mark was saying with a bright smile at Jill, as if they were all on the same page.

"More homes mean more groceries, Mark," Jill grumbled under her breath as she stomped on toward Arnie's.

"You're right. They're only interested in meeting me because I'm your husband." Vince's words dripped with sarcasm.

"Shut up." Great. Now he'd gotten her to resort to

school-yard retorts. "What happened back there when the car backfired?"

"It just took me out of my game, is all," Vince said smoothly. "When's the last time someone in this town got a new car—1975?"

"Contrary to what you think," she said, "cars are not fashion accessories."

"I've never seen such a collection of clunkers."

Jill waved off his insinuation. "I know it's hard for you to understand the concept of being thrifty. People get new cars when they need them." But it *was* odd that she hadn't seen anyone with an up-to-date vehicle in a long, long time.

"Jill, the average income in Railroad Stop is below the poverty line. As mayor, aren't you supposed to be improving the standard of living?"

"I am, remember? Vacation homes? Golf course?" Jill walked faster. "But I'm also about integrity and preserving the heart of the town." Jill wasn't interested in what other people thought they needed. If they wanted a different life, there were plenty of cookie-cutter towns in the California foothills. Railroad Stop was special.

"It's amazing you won the election." Vince watched a car pull onto Main Street.

Jill bared her teeth as she tried to smile.

"JILL, WHAT A SURPRISE." Arnie held open the door to the Railroad Stop Museum and Pizzeria. His smile for Jill was smooth as glass, more than friendly, and it set Vince's teeth on edge.

With a wary nod, Jill gave Arnie a wide berth and

headed quickly past him toward the back of the foyer, her ponytail barely swaying. Arnie watched her every step of the way, sending Vince's proprietary gene into overdrive. It could have been a power play, designed to get under Vince's skin.

Vince flexed his fingers. Recognizing the ploy didn't make it any easier to take. Maybe there was more to being married than Vince was ready to admit. Or perhaps he was just sensitive to attack, given his grandfather's terse e-mail demanding an update on the project.

"Mr. Patrizio." Arnie looked less like a local and more like a Silicon Valley millionaire in his dress slacks and button-down shirt. He gave Vince's Podunky clothing a surprised once-over, but didn't immediately run screaming from the room.

Vince tugged at the long sleeves of the shirt. Needing a moment to compose himself, he took his time shaking Arnie's hand and looking around the old house that served as Railroad Stop's repository of history. There were hardwood floors, faded oriental carpets, high windows with heavy draperies and small tufted chairs that looked as if they'd break under Vince's weight. A display case with an Indian headdress, a few arrowheads and woven baskets flanked the staircase. Black-and-white photos of early settlers hung on the wall—scruffy miners, women in long skirts and aprons, Native Americans of every age and gender.

Arnie put a stop to Vince's perusal with a huff. "I want you to meet one of our tribal elders, Mildred Jones." Arnie drew Vince farther into the museum.

The woman with the silver Princess Leia braids they'd encountered on the road sat primly in a chair wearing a long jean skirt and calico blouse. Vince shook her bony hand and was surprised at her firm grip.

"Mildred says you were posting signs against the casino, Vince." Arnie shot Jill a reproachful look. "I told her that couldn't be."

Smiling, the mayor—*his wife*—cocked an eyebrow.

"It's true," Vince admitted.

"Posting signs that could kill our project?" Arnie opened his mouth as if he'd like to say more, but then his gaze shifted again to Jill. The tribal leader snapped his mouth closed and the room fell into a painful silence.

Jill smirked at Vince, reveling in his impending failure.

Vince smiled right back. This was going to be her payback for not telling him she was the mayor. "You're missing the point, Arnie. This isn't about dividing a community. It's about uniting it. Everyone should have a voice." Vince smiled at Mildred and then winked at Jill. He may have blown seven deals, but with each loss he'd learned something he was going to use in Railroad Stop.

Bobbing her head, Mildred's lined blue eyes sparkled.

Arnie stared at Vince and then his frown fell away as he laughed in that slow, heavy way of his. "You're exactly right."

Jill's mouth hung open. Vince would have bet she wanted to set the record straight—that she'd bamboozled and bullied Vince into helping—but any argument Jill had would only make her look bad. Just in case, Vince decided it was time for a change in subject.

Vince crossed the foyer to the door marked Pizza. "Let's talk, Arnie. Do you think the restaurant can fit us in during the lunch-hour rush?"

"I can see why you married him, dear. He's a keeper," Mildred said to Jill. "Why, if I were twenty years younger and you decided you didn't want him..."

The rest of Mildred's comment was lost because Arnie drew Vince through the door into the pizza parlor just as two teenagers wearing red polo shirts completed a pass with a Frisbee across the deserted dining area. Seeing Arnie, they dashed behind the counter, stowing the plastic disk beneath it.

Vince looked around the newer addition and then checked his watch. Twelve-thirty on a Saturday was lunchtime in most places he knew.

"Let's sit down. Jimmy, bring us two waters." Arnie led Vince over to a wooden picnic table that had various names and messages carved in its top. "You had me worried when Mildred told me about the signs."

Instead of answering, Vince took another inventory of the place—outdated video games, gumball and sticky hand dispensers. The only thing missing was beer posters.

"I know what you're thinking." Arnie interrupted Vince's perusal. "How can a town like Railroad Stop support an Indian casino when they can barely support a pizza place?"

"Or a gas station, bakery and grocery store," Vince added.

The taller of the teenagers put two red plastic tumblers filled with water in front of them.

"Vince Patrizio, I'd like you to meet my nephew, Jimmy." Arnie's voice glowed with pride.

"Nice to meet you." Despite goofing off just a few minutes earlier, Jimmy had a strong handshake and met Vince's gaze squarely even as Vince noticed a long silver scar running from Jimmy's left elbow to his wrist.

The teen caught him looking and shrugged, for the first time showing a more typical teenager's indifference. "My dad was fond of knives. Would you like a pizza? Or some buffalo wings?"

"Water's fine for now, Jimmy." Arnie dismissed him.

"Nice meeting you," Jimmy said coolly before returning to the counter.

"My brother..." Arnie glanced back at Jimmy. "When there isn't a lot of hope or opportunity...well, it's far too easy for some to develop bad habits or inappropriate attitudes."

Vince realized there were no beer taps, no wine displays. The evidence that there once had been was standing behind the counter glaring at him. The way Jimmy didn't hide his scars unsettled Vince. As far as Vince was concerned, the past should remain your own private business. Vince rubbed his arm and then sucked down more water.

"People are our greatest resource." Arnie's voice dropped to a near whisper. "And yet can be our greatest obstacle."

"Is he...is your brother in jail?"

"Yes." Arnie stared at the ice cubes floating in his glass. "I ran a successful business in Silicon Valley, but my brother could see no farther than his next can of beer. He understood why I had to send him away." Arnie's face seemed carved out of stone. "He wanted me to raise Jimmy here."

Vince gave a tight nod as he pretended interest in

the sign for Railroad Stop's annual father-son river-rafting trip, being held tomorrow.

"As you can imagine, there aren't many job opportunities in town for our youth. The few positions available go to the older citizens, who have experience. By keeping the pizza parlor open I can give the kids job skills, teach them about customer service, how to work a register and the value of showing up to work prepared and on time."

"But not everyone can do that." Not everyone had made a giant nest egg in the dot.com industry. This was the first indication that the project might not be such a good idea and Vince didn't like it. "You said on the phone that you had tourist traffic here."

"It's sporadic," Arnie admitted, still not back to his blustery self. "Mostly seasonal. Folks northeast of Sacramento pass by on their way to ski in the winter. We're a gateway to outdoor activities in the summer and fall—rafting, fishing, camping, hunting. A casino would increase our traffic year-round."

"That's a big order for any business."

"Our children either self-destruct or leave. Our heritage will die if we don't do something." He met Vince's stare. "I'm willing to put up the tribe's stake in this. We will succeed."

Vince didn't doubt it. He snuck a glance at Jimmy, who noticed and scowled. "Have you sat down and talked to Jill about this?"

Arnie waved away the question as if shooing off a fly. "She doesn't want to listen. Her boy is too young yet for her to understand. Besides, Jill thinks vacation homes are the answer when they'll only stretch the divide between the haves and the have-nots."

"But the profits from the casino will go to the tribe, not anyone else in town," Vince felt compelled to point out, even though it was something Jill had said last night.

"We'll contribute tax dollars from casino profits and payroll taxes."

"But nothing directly to the town? Nothing to help the rest of the businesses here?"

"We're an *Indian* casino. The foremost beneficiaries are Native Americans."

Vince nodded, but it was more a polite indication that he'd heard the words than an agreement.

Arnie's gaze dropped and he wiped condensation from his glass with his thumb. "I'd like to review the architectural drawings with you Monday morning. I loaned them to the last holdout from the tribal council last night. Once you've seen them you'll understand that the Railroad Stop Indian Casino will be a destination, not a drive-by attraction."

"Sure. Come up to Shady Oak."

"So, you're staying there," Arnie said. "How's it going with your…with the mayor?"

"She'll come around," Vince replied, knowing it was a lie.

Arnie chuckled again and pounded Vince on the back. "I knew what that girl needed was a man."

"None of that, Arnie, please." Jill's voice was calm but there were two bright spots of color on her cheeks as she stood in the doorway. She spun her wedding ring with her left thumb.

Jill used that ring like a force field to keep men

away. She might have suggested divorce, but he didn't believe Jill really wanted—

"Are you finished? I need to get back." Jill disappeared without waiting for Vince's response.

Vince was struck by an idea that his grandfather, a master manipulator, would be proud of. He needed the mayor in his back pocket.

"Sorry about that," Arnie said, grinning without a bit of remorse, as if he enjoyed pushing Jill's buttons.

Absently, Vince arranged a time to meet with Arnie Monday morning and hurried to catch up with Jill, pausing at the door to look back at Jimmy, who gave him a defiant stare, his left arm bare for everyone to see, to comment on, to ask about.

Vince turned away.

Things in Railroad Stop were becoming too personal. Vince sucked at personal.

CHAPTER NINE

VINCE HAD TURNED the tables on Jill. Again. And then he had the nerve to reassure Arnie that she'd come around? She of all people? Agree with Arnie? *Never!*

"Can I help you, Mildred?" Jill asked, hesitating outside the museum when she'd rather be hauling tush back to her office without Vince. But there was Mildred, struggling to get her SUV's door open.

"I'm fine, dear. The lock sticks every once in a while, that's all." Half bent, Mildred contorted her frail body, as the tried to turn the key in the lock.

"Here. Let me. I'm good at fixing things." Vince brushed past Jill, leaving her swaying toward him like a branch in the wind.

The man was a bundle of pheromones, a tempting lure Jill had problems ignoring. "And if you believe that I've got a bridge to sell you," Jill mumbled.

With a glance over his shoulder, Vince hesitated at the windshield before turning to Mildred. Then he did a double take. "Is that a dog in the driver's seat?"

"Oh, that." Mildred giggled. "That's Horace. He's my antitheft device."

"He's huge." Vince peered through the front of the car. "Is he a...monkey?"

"Yes," Mildred preened, clearly under the effect of Vince's spell. She didn't see that Vince had the power to destroy her quiet, predictable life. "I won him at the state fair several years back knocking down milk jugs. I was an all-state pitcher in my day. I still work out. Want to feel my muscle?" She flexed one stringy arm.

"Ah…how about I try your key, instead?" Keeping his distance, Vince held out his hand.

"You young men don't know what you're missin'." With a shake of her silver earmuff hairdo, Mildred gave Vince the key. "Have you looked at your man's shoulders, Jill? You don't see shoulders like that around here very often. Don't you just love being held by such a hunky guy?"

Jill declined to take the bait. Vince's shoulders were rather nice, but strong shoulders meant an ability to control and overpower a woman. It was bad enough they were locked in this battle of wits.

Unaware of Jill's thoughts, Vince rolled his eyes in Jill's direction. "Mildred, do you know Edda Mae?"

Mildred beamed. "She's my best friend. Has been since third grade. Why?"

"I don't know. Something about the way you talk about me—almost as if I wasn't there." He fiddled with the key in the lock until it screeched in protest and clicked. Vince opened the door, peered in and then turned back to Mildred. "A steering-wheel lock? I thought Horace was your antitheft device."

"You can't be too careful. I'll have you know—" Mildred put her nose in the air "—this was one of the first SUVs ever built. It's a classic and has always been a target of thieves."

"That's what I heard, too," Vince said, gifting Mildred with a charming smile that had her bubbling her thanks.

The vermin. Clearly he'd hatched some kind of demented plan with Arnie, and it involved humiliating Jill in front of each one of her constituents.

And Vince kept right on smiling as he hopped up onto the wood-plank sidewalk next to Jill.

Bidding Mildred goodbye, Jill started walking at a clip designed to leave Vince in her dust.

"So…we learned something today. You, the *mayor,* don't want a casino," Vince said, easily catching up to Jill.

"Uh-huh." Jill walked faster.

"Arnie, the tribal leader, wants a casino and you, but probably wants the casino more."

"Arnie wants Shady Oak. Since he couldn't buy it…" She shrugged, wondering where this was leading.

"No interest in Arnie? He's not husband material?"

"Arnie?" She made a disgusted noise. "I'm not divorcing you to marry Arnie, if that's what you're getting at."

"Just making sure." Without breaking stride, Vince bent closer and spoke into her ear, sending heat where he had no right to send it. "I have a proposition for you."

"Two in one day? How does a girl get so lucky?" Jill felt rather breathless, but that could have been because she was walking so fast.

"This is one you'll find very interesting, *wife.*" He caught Jill's arm.

Jill's heart pounded double-time as warmth radiated from his hand. She couldn't help but think that if this was her Vince, the Vince she'd daydreamed about for years, she'd turn and fall into his arms, welcome his waiting kiss and confirm in no uncertain terms that she didn't want a divorce or Arnie.

But this wasn't her Vince, as evidenced by the way he led her into the shade of a narrow alley, fenced her against a wall behind the local gift shop's cypress bush and tilted her chin up so that she had no choice but to look him in the eye.

"I learned something else about you today." He gave her the smallest of grins. "You don't want a divorce."

"I—I do want a divorce," Jill stammered.

Vince shook his head sadly. "No, you don't. I may be a pretty boy with nice shoulders," Vince said, reminding her of Edda Mae's and Mildred's assessments. The intensity of his black gaze ignited something he had no right to ignite while Jill was dreading…contemplating divorce. "You accused me of using our marriage to keep women at a distance emotionally, but you use our marriage and that ring of yours like a security fence—to keep men away physically."

There was no reason to answer. He was right. She licked her lips, unwittingly drawing his attention to her mouth.

Vince was near enough that panic skittered along Jill's nerves—not that he seemed to care. All she had to do was lift a hand to touch him. Part of her begged for space, for freedom, while the rest of her pleaded to close the distance between them.

"I can give you back what Craig took away." After a moment's hesitation Vince stroked Jill's cheek with the back of his hand, the warm metal of his wedding band sending a delicious shiver that shortcircuited her brain. "You'd like that, wouldn't you? Then you wouldn't need this—" his fingers found hers and spun her wedding ring in a languorous circle "—or me."

But Jill *did* need Vince. Jill trembled from wanting him to touch her, yearning for him to work that magic with those lips of his. If only she wouldn't freak out when he did.

Unable to take it anymore, Jill closed her eyes.

"All you have to do is reach out—" his warm breath drifted over her ear, tauntingly magnetic "—and take me."

Could it be that easy? Could she trust him?

"Jill?" Vince held himself back, kept himself from claiming Jill with the contact he craved.

He was no fool. As soon as he made his offer—an idea that had come to him in the pizza parlor earlier— Jill would never let him near her again. And who could blame her? He was going to use Jill, as his grandfather had used hundreds of others in his quest to seal a deal. It didn't matter that the result would justify the means. There was little hope Vince could make Jill believe in the casino. The only way to garner her loyalty was to deal for it and hope she was desperate enough to take the bait.

So he stood mere inches away from Jill and waited for her answer, aching to kiss her one last time. He didn't expect her to take up his challenge, because she didn't have the courage to reach for him. Unlike Vince, Jill lacked the nerve to risk everything for something she wanted.

Jill's unexpected touch on his arm shocked Vince backward. If she hadn't grabbed his shirt, he might have fallen. Jill's face drained of color as she took in his surprise. She tried to shove him back, but Vince's feet were planted on the ground.

"You tried to kiss me," Vince blurted, still stunned.

Jill backed against the wall, fists clenched, cheeks a bright red. "Don't play with me like that. I want you off my property *today*." She wound her arm back as if to slap him.

Vince captured her wrist. "It's not like that."

"Isn't it? You told me you'd do anything to make this deal happen. Since I'm about the only person standing in your way, I'd like to know. What is it you're going to use against me? *Sex*." She whispered the word, her gaze slipping away.

He let her go. "Jill..."

"So the rest...about Craig. That was just you toying with me."

"No. I wouldn't do that to you." It was weird. He cared for Jill and he wanted her to be happy, but that didn't stop Vince from using her if it was to his advantage. He was the ultimate jerk and he was consumed with second thoughts, but what if she agreed...

Something in the way Vince looked at Jill must have given him away, because she didn't back down. Her eyes narrowed dangerously. "So, what's this proposition?"

Don't tell her. Don't say it. Don't—

"Marriage." Vince's dry mouth had difficulty forming the word. "If what you want is to continue business as usual, we can stay married the way we have been— just as friends."

He'd struck a chord. Some of the fire left Jill for just a moment. Then she frowned. "In exchange for...?"

Jill was forcing Vince to say it, making him squirm like the snake she thought he was. "You'll always feel safe wearing my ring. I'll stay married to you—if you support this casino deal."

She slapped him.

But as Vince followed Jill back to the truck, he held on to one thought: she hadn't turned him down.

"EDDA MAE'S CRYING again." Teddy met the truck at the top of the driveway, standing on his toes to hang on Jill's open window.

"I'll take care of it," Jill assured Teddy, fairly certain she knew what was bothering Edda Mae.

As soon as Jill parked Edda Mae's truck, Vince opened his door, but Jill threw her arm across his chest. She hadn't spoken to him since he'd made her his *oh-so-generous* offer. He was probably wondering why she hadn't given him an answer.

Jill was pondering her options. If she took the high road, kicked him out and divorced him and somehow managed to foil his plans, someone else was bound to come along with more charm and more money. If she accepted his deal, she'd be in on the negotiations with Arnie and perhaps be able to convince them of the folly of a casino. But accepting Vince's offer meant that temptation, in the form of Vince, remained. Vince recognized that Jill was attracted to him and was just playing with her emotions. Jill wasn't sure how much more she could take. In the end, there was no choice.

"I'll handle this. If you want to help—" ha! as if Vince could help "—keep Teddy occupied…while you pack. I'm going to take you up on your proposal, but only if you move out and keep me in the meetings loop on the casino. It wasn't fair of you to run out with Arnie earlier."

"No way." Vince rubbed his cheek, reminding her he'd taken the last hit. "I either stay here or all deals are null and void."

"I can't agree to your terms." Jill didn't wait for Vince to comment, but popped out her side of the truck. "Which bungalow, Teddy?"

"Nine." Teddy pointed to one of the most remote cabins.

Edda Mae was putting a rocking chair through its paces on the porch of Bungalow Nine, a tissue crumpled in one fist and Moonbeam curled in a tight ball in her lap.

Balancing her rump on the railing across from the older woman, Jill settled in. Sometimes it took several minutes for Edda Mae to feel like talking.

"Francie called," Edda Mae woefully admitted after a while, staring off into the distance. "Little Maria came down with the chicken pox, so Francie had to miss work again."

Francie meant well when she called her mother, but their conversations generally drove Edda Mae to tears. This time with good reason. There was nothing as upsetting as mommy guilt. Or in this case grandmommy guilt.

"You could go," Jill suggested softly, her brain snapping through coping scenarios. A group from a credit union in the valley was checking in tomorrow. How could Jill possibly run the three-day event without Edda Mae? There would be laundry and dishes and cooking, not to mention guests to be schmoozed.

"When Francie moved away, I always thought it was temporary, that she'd come back." Edda Mae sniffed. "When she called to tell me she was pregnant I could barely breathe, I was that certain she'd tell me she was finally coming home." Edda Mae stroked Moonbeam's snowy fluff.

"I know," Jill acknowledged gently.

"Generations of my family have lived here. Look at these trees." Edda Mae gestured weakly at the pines twenty feet beyond the cabin. "Those trees are older than I am. Who knows what they've seen. How could Francie leave all that history behind?"

"She went to college. That's something a mother should be proud of." But suddenly Jill didn't want Teddy to go off to school. He was all she had. If he left…Jill didn't want to think about it, more so because it opened the floodgates to Vince's casino arguments.

"*Pah,* who needs college. You didn't go and look how well you've done. All college does is seduce you with technology and crowds and…" Edda Mae's face crumpled. "She's never coming back, is she?"

Jill knelt at the foot of the rocker and covered one of Edda Mae's hands with her own. "She might." If Vince opened a casino in Railroad Stop, there'd be a finance job Francie was qualified for. Maybe she should agree to the deal with Vince. But Railroad Stop—and Jill—would never be the same and neither would the experience she could offer guests at Shady Oak. "Why don't you take some time off? Go help Francie take care of Maria? You could leave Monday morning and come back Sunday."

The day after the credit union checked out, a

group of nuns was checking in. They were spending their time at Shady Oak under a vow of silence and paying a heavily discounted rate for simple food, peace and quiet.

There was a flash of hope in the older woman's eyes that quickly faded. "Who would cook for you?"

"I have your recipe book. And Teddy." She'd manage. Somehow.

"Loyalty is built through the belly," Edda Mae countered staunchly.

"Last week you said my biscuits came out well."

"Humph."

"And lasagna. I can make lasagna." If Jill made a quick trip down the hill to Costco, she could pick up a couple of frozen trays of—

"If you so much as breathe the words *frozen food*, I'll chain myself to the stove." Edda Mae knew Jill too well.

Jill had to think fast. If Edda Mae wanted to go, Jill would find a way to make it happen. "I could do a baked-potato bar the first night and barbecue burgers the second."

Edda Mae shook her head. "What was I thinking? You can't cook, clean the rooms and run things, not by yourself." She brightened. "What about Vince?"

"He's leaving." Jill hoped he was packing as they spoke. She'd have to divorce him. She just…didn't want to tell him yet. Jill touched her ring with her left thumb.

Edda Mae's gaze was piercing. "You don't know what you have there, Jill. He's a good man. He's—"

"Leaving," Jill said, hoping it was true. "I'll find someone in town to help me. I'm a big girl, Edda Mae. I can do this."

"You said the same thing when you wanted to buy the place."

"Well, you sold it to me in the end, didn't you? I love you, Edda Mae, but you've got to come to terms with Francie's choice." Or make one of her own. It would be just Jill's luck to have Edda Mae decide to move closer to her daughter at a time she needed her mentor the most.

"We didn't get all the bungalows clean." Edda Mae frowned. "Or put out the clean linens."

"I'll take care of it." Jill knew there was a ton of work ahead of her, but this was so clearly what Edda Mae needed to do. "Why don't you go get ready? I'll finish wiping down the cabins. It's been a busy morning—you might want to rest, too."

"There you go again, saying I'm old and useless. That means you owe me a hug." Edda Mae set Moonbeam down, then stood and enfolded Jill fiercely in her arms. "Someday you'll realize that you need a man. I just hope you get smart before you let this one get away. I'd bet my dentures he loves you."

There was undeniable chemistry between them. But love? Jill didn't think Vince knew the meaning of the word. "I wouldn't make that bet. It'll be awfully hard to gum down your food."

UPDATE ME on Indian casino ASAP.

Vince leaned against the fender of his Porsche and reread the message from his grandfather. Not that his grandfather had typed it. Aldo Patrizio dictated most of his missives from his wife's bedside, and his assistant keyed them into the computer. There was no postscript about Vince's grandmother's condition, no warm closing. That type of correspondence had ended months ago, taking with it most of Vince's hope that they might reconcile.

Vince wanted to talk to his grandfather and ask him his opinion of this deal. The profit potential was in question, as was the impact on the local community. But given their rocky relationship, Vince was sure his grandfather would laugh and call him weak. He'd certainly used the word to describe Vince enough times before.

His thumbs hesitated over the minute keyboard, held immobile by indecision. Where did his loyalties lie? Jill hated him—and for good reason, much as he tried not to care. His grandfather considered him dead weight. And Arnie was starting to doubt Vince's dedication to the project.

Vince returned the BlackBerry to his belt clip, e-mail unanswered. Since there was no signal here, whatever he wrote he wouldn't be able to send, so to reply was useless. And he wasn't ready to call using a landline. He needed time to think the situation over.

"Hey, Teddy, what are you doing?" Vince asked, having spotted Teddy upstairs in the far corner of the back porch. Vince took the stairs two at a time to join him.

Teddy's toes were on the bottom rail of the second-story landing, his arms draped over the top one. "I'm painting." A sturdy wooden easel had been set up on the porch, hovering over Teddy's work gloves and ski mask.

"Hmm." Vince took a closer look. The paper on the easel was blank. Then he followed Teddy's gaze. From the upper deck they had a good view of the slope leading down to a bit of road and the tribal land. The air was still clear and fresh after the rain, but there was nothing much for a boy to be staring at. "Painting what?"

"I don't know yet."

Vince checked his watch. "When will you know?"

"Soon, I hope." Teddy rested his chin on his fist. "Have you ever gone rafting?"

"No."

A small gray bird swooped below them.

"I have. It's a lot of fun. This is the last weekend for it because the river water is so low."

Comprehension dawned. "Ah, the father-son rafting trip."

Angling his head to the side, Teddy breathed longingly, "Yes."

"I suppose a lot of your friends are going."

"Yes." That same longing.

Vince knew when he was being played. He wished he could satisfy the boy's unspoken request, but he doubted Jill would let him.

With a sigh Teddy turned back to the easel. "I think I'll paint now."

"You've decided on something, have you?"

Teddy picked up the brush and dipped it in the blue paint. "I think I'll paint the Mokelumne River."

Of course. Vince forced the corners of his mouth down.

Another dramatic sigh. "And then maybe I'll add a rafter or two." With his brush, Teddy traced a sharply twisting line diagonally across the page.

Unable to hold back his laughter any longer, Vince waited until Teddy put the brush down to explain. "If you want to go on the rafting trip, why don't you just ask?"

Before Vince knew what hit him, Teddy had thrown down his brush and leaped into Vince's arms. "Oh, thank you, thank you, thank you."

"I didn't say I could take you." Vince sobered. "We'll have to ask—"

"Mom." Teddy slid down and went back to the railing. "Forget it. She'll say no."

Even though Vince tended to agree, he couldn't let Teddy give up. "Why don't we ask her tonight at dinner?"

"You *are* Batman." Teddy launched himself back at Vince. "Thank you, thank you, thank you."

The boy could thank Vince all he wanted, but that didn't mean Jill was going to let them go.

"If I'm Batman—" Vince was starting to feel like the Dark Knight, breaking the rules to make things right "—then you must be…"

Teddy stared at Vince, anxiously awaiting his pronouncement.

"Teddy, this is where you say which superhero you want to be." It was another boy ritual.

"Uh, Spiderman?"

"He's good. He could definitely kick Batman's butt, but not Superman's."

There was hero worship—for Vince—in Teddy's eyes.

"Okay, Teddy. It's your turn to come up with a match-up. You know, Superman couldn't beat…"

"Harry Potter?" Teddy laughed much too hard.

"You have no idea how to do this, do you?" Vince asked.

Teddy shook his head. "The boys at school do it, but…" He shrugged.

"Your education is sadly lacking." And while Teddy painted, Vince clued him in on more secret rituals of boys.

CHAPTER TEN

"I THOUGHT you'd have left by now," Jill snapped at Vince when she dragged herself in the door several hours later. He was a nice piece of eye candy, but Jill was too exhausted to be on guard tonight.

She had missed lunch, but the bungalows were clean and ready for guests. Edda Mae had helped her hang towels and stock the rooms with toiletries. Now she faced a dilemma—what to make for dinner when all she wanted to do was collapse on her bed.

Except something smelled wonderful.

And Vince was still here.

"Why don't you go get cleaned up? Edda Mae put a casserole in this afternoon." Vince was in the kitchen chopping green pepper by the salad bowl, wielding the large knife as if he knew how to use it. The casserole was steaming on top of the stove.

Jill wanted Vince gone. She filled her nose with the spicy, warm scent of food. Her stomach rumbled.

She could deal with him after dinner.

"What have you two been doing all day?"

"We…um…I…painted and did my silent reading." Teddy waved a book at her and spun in his chair to face her, his smile forced.

Jill's mommy radar went off. Something wasn't right here. Her birthday was months away, as was Christmas. And yet Teddy was hiding something. She scanned the living room, but nothing appeared broken or missing.

Finally she fixed Teddy with her best no-nonsense look. "Teddy—"

"Teddy's a smart kid." Vince tossed the salad as if it required most of his attention, as if unaware Jill was trying to interrogate her son.

A muscle in Jill's jaw jumped. Vince knew what Teddy was hiding. She waited patiently for someone to cave in. Teddy didn't usually last long under her look, but he was still fiddling with his book. Jill's glare ricocheted between the two.

"Dinner's in five. Just need to take out the rolls." Vince wouldn't look at Jill. "Why don't you go clean up?"

The food smelled delicious. Jill was starving, but she held her ground.

"I'll set the table." As if on cue, Teddy popped up to help without being asked.

Jill narrowed her eyes at the two males of the species. Cooking dinner? Setting the table? They wanted something. Yet they said nothing, asked for nothing. Finally Jill gave up and went to change into something that didn't smell of bug spray and disinfectant. She could unravel whatever was going on after she ate.

They made their move during dinner.

"What do you have planned for Teddy tomorrow?" Vince asked, dishing out his second helping of chicken-and-cheesy-rice casserole.

"Teddy's our gopher." Jill grimaced. She wasn't

breaking any child-labor laws. They ran a family business. Teddy helped out in the few ways he could. "It's an important job."

"I thought…I mean, I heard…" It wasn't like Vince to hesitate. He glanced at Teddy, who made a go-for-it move with his eyebrows.

"Just spill it," Jill said, trying to ignore the knot in her lower back.

"All the kids are going rafting tomorrow and I want to go, too," Teddy blurted, pushing his plate away and standing. He produced a folded, wrinkled sheet of paper from his jeans pocket. He flattened out the creases and thrust it at her. "I downloaded the form from the Internet. I need your signature on this permission slip and twenty dollars to rent the raft."

Jill gathered her dirty dishes. "I'll take you rafting another day."

Teddy let the paper fall onto the table. "No. It's the father-son rafting trip." He propped his hands on his hips and posed like Superman. All Teddy needed was a cape, some height and a few muscles.

Father-son? Jill slouched in her chair. "But who…?" Jill's mouth snapped shut. She knew who.

"We're going." Teddy gestured between Vince and himself. "No moms allowed."

Now all Teddy's urgency about a father made sense.

Vince shrugged under Jill's withering stare. "Teddy really wants to go."

Damn Vince. "Teddy never wanted to go before." Before Vince barged into their lives with his own personal agenda and ruined the peaceful environment she'd created.

"I never asked before because I didn't know I had a dad then." The mutinous curl to Teddy's lip left no doubt that Jill needed a bulletproof reason why Teddy shouldn't go.

But she had no reason to ban Teddy from attending other than her distrust of Vince. He wasn't the man of her dreams any longer; therefore, he wasn't good enough to play the role of father. Unfortunately she had no one else to send Teddy with.

"He's not your father." Jill forced the words past stiff lips.

"He's my stepdad. That's almost the real thing." Teddy beamed at Vince with misplaced hero worship.

Jill wanted to strangle Vince. She could live with her fears when she divorced Vince, but if Vince won Teddy over, his young heart would be broken. It was bad enough Vince was here, but to offer to take her son on the rafting trip? He had to have some ulterior motive.

As if reading her mind, Vince raised his hands in surrender. "No strings."

Just the fact that Vince guessed what Jill was thinking annoyed her. "Teddy, start clearing the table please. I need to talk to Vince."

"I want to go." Teddy glared at Jill, giving her a glimpse of the mutinous teenager she'd never expected him to be. "With Vince."

"And I said no."

"You're going to tell him he can't take me." Teddy's lip started to tremble. He stomped into the kitchen with his plate.

"Teddy—" Jill wasn't sure if she spoke in warning or to soothe.

"Big boys who do chores," Teddy called from the kitchen, "get allowances and vacations."

"I give you an allowance." Jill refused to look at Vince.

"And they get to buy what they want. Like video games." He'd worked himself up to near max volume.

"No video games. They dull your mind and desensitize you to reality." She'd said the same thing to Teddy a hundred times before and thought he'd understood. But that was before Vince, who was looking at her as if she was from another planet and he was considering blasting her to smithereens with his ray gun.

"They don't," Teddy said mutinously. "They're fun."

"Teddy, you don't know—"

"I played them at my friend's house before. And today Vince let me play his."

Jill scanned the area by the television for a game system, but she didn't see any wires or consoles. Then she caught Vince's glance at the desk. Jill stood and walked over. Teddy's book was on top of something. She lifted it to reveal a black plastic rectangle, smaller than most eyeglass cases. Jill held it up.

"I didn't know," Vince said, reaching for the portable video game quickly, as if afraid she'd hurl it at him.

"Don't bother," Teddy said. "I'm her slave and she doesn't want me to have any friends or any fun." He ran into his room and slammed the door.

Jill had to sit down. Her little boy. Her baby. She'd been so careful raising him. And in one afternoon Vince had turned Teddy against her.

"It's not enough that you have to ruin Railroad Stop. You have to sabotage my home life, too?"

"If you're trying to blame what Craig did to you on

video games, this is going to take a lot longer to sort out." Vince's voice was calm.

Jill shot out of her seat. "You don't know what you're talking about." Silverware clanked onto plates as she began clearing the table, sorely tempted to dump what was left of Teddy's milk on Vince's head. Instead, she stomped into the kitchen much as Teddy had done earlier, dumping the dishes none too gently into the sink.

"Don't I?" Vince followed her with the casserole dish. "You've had a lot of time up here to think about that night. You've probably tried to put the pieces together like one of those mystery shows, tried to figure out what in Craig's history made him such a predator." Vince blocked Jill in the corner of the kitchen with a hand on either counter. "What did you come up with besides video games? Football? Money? Listen, Jill, his father treated his mother like shit. Rumors were that his mother had one hell of a drug habit. One night his father beat her to death and then shot himself. He probably would have killed Craig if he'd been in the house."

Jill blinked back the tears as she shook her head slowly. "Please say you're just making that up." She didn't want to feel sorry for Craig.

Large palms settled on her shoulders. "It's the truth. They had money. They looked like they had everything. But Craig's parents screwed up his head, not MTV or video games. Craig didn't have anyone stable in his life."

Taking a risk, Jill hooked her fingers on Vince's wrists as something bitter inside her eased, then calmed further when he didn't pull away. She closed her eyes. She'd been driven by resentment so long her knees almost gave way with relief. Involuntarily, her grip on Vince solidified, her need for support so desperate that she'd hold on to the one man with the power to take her down.

And yet, unlike Craig, the abuse Vince had suffered at the hands of his father hadn't made Vince into a monster. Vince might be a lot of things, but he wasn't cruel like Craig. It would have been easier to believe the school rebel was the one to fear, but Jill knew better. "Somehow I think you would have turned out all right even if your grandparents *hadn't* taken you in."

Jill opened her eyes and looked at Vince, into dark eyes that held all the tenderness she'd needed at eighteen. Jill was filled with a yearning to be gutsy or sexy or at least normal, so that kissing Vince would seem as natural as breathing.

"I want to kiss you," he whispered, as if they were teenagers and they were going through their first chaste embrace.

"I know," she whispered back, clinging to the notion that they were two innocents embarking on this together.

His lips dropped closer. "I'm going to kiss you."

"You talk way too much."

Vince paused, a hair's breadth from her mouth. "You can stop me at any time."

His beautiful eyes were nearly black, languid, brimming with a longing that almost did Jill in. She pressed her lips to his, emboldened by the power he was giving her. She could end this at any time.

But she didn't want to.

His lips were soft and warm, and his hands remained

on her shoulders ready to catch her if she stumbled back. Only, she didn't. She pressed herself closer until her breasts came up against his chest. As he drew in a shuddering breath, filling his lungs with air, Jill shifted minutely, creating a delicious friction between them. Her nipples hardened and her body throbbed.

Vince continued to kiss her with a tenderness that simultaneously soothed and urged. And Jill continued to shift her body, increasing the friction between them. The need to touch Vince this way became more insistent, her movements more desperate. Her breath hitched. Her breasts tingled. More. She needed more....

Vince groaned softly against her lips, rotating his head from side to side as if she was torturing him, which was crazy. He was torturing her just by standing there and letting her touch him. And then Vince sucked her lower lip into his mouth.

Jill stretched up toward Vince reflexively, bringing her hips against his. For one moment she felt a burst of pleasure *down there* from the rigidness of his body against hers. And then she realized she was pressing herself shamelessly against his erection.

"Stop." Jill crumpled back against the counter, unable to look above the yoke of blue plaid that covered Vince's chest, torn between wanting to continue her fully-clothed exploration of his body and panic that bad things would happen if she went too far. And it would be all her fault.

"Okay." A terse acknowledgment of her command. Vince still held her shoulders, his wrists still encompassed by Jill's hands. And then he added a softer, breathier, "Okay."

The battery-operated wall clock hummed. They stood below it in the corner of the kitchen, thankfully out of sight of Teddy, should he decide to open his door and shout some more. If he came into the living room, though, he'd see them. And yet, Jill couldn't move. Her body was a tangle of longing, and there was an intimacy to the moment she was reluctant to end.

Jill raised her eyes in wonder as she became aware of something. "Are you trembling, or is that me?"

His smile was strained. "It's me."

"I did that to you?" And he hadn't ripped her clothes off and forced himself on her?

"By God, you did." Vince sounded breathless. "And I'd let you do it again. Anytime. Even if it's only for one night."

Jill's cheeks heated. "Even if I...even if you couldn't..."

"Even if *we* couldn't," Vince confirmed, lowering his forehead until it touched hers.

Flies could have navigated easily into Jill's mouth, it was that widely ajar. There was no way the man in front of her was Vince Patrizio. He wanted Jill to believe he'd make do with third base?

Teddy's door opened. "I'm brushing my teeth and going to bed."

The bathroom door slammed. The fan came on.

She supposed she'd have to let Teddy go on the father-son rafting trip.

Teddy, who'd been under Vince's spell and conveniently broken rules he knew by heart. Jill couldn't blame it all on Vince. He didn't have kids. He wouldn't know to check with a parent before exposing a child to a new food, a movie rated above G or—the biggie—video games.

Wait a minute. Jill blinked. She was under Vince's spell, too. A marriage between friends?

"You almost had me," she said, slipping past Vince, turning to face him from the other side of the kitchen. "What? Because I didn't take you up on the offer, you tried Plan B? You disgust me. All deals are off."

SHE'LL NEVER trust me.

Vince pounded down the stairs into the black night in search of air. He couldn't blame Jill. No. This mess was all of his own making. He should have treated her as a business associate from the start, not let himself get caught up in this attraction.

Long strides and the bite of cold air did nothing to ease the sting of impending failure. He was so close to forging a deal he could taste it. And yet, he couldn't deny the feeling that he needed Jill to make it happen. Vince found himself heading up the trail he and Jill had taken this morning when he'd kissed her the first time.

When had he lost sight of his goals? How could he have kissed Jill twice when so much was on the line?

Maybe I love her.

Vince halted, his feet firmly on the ground. He didn't do love. This was about lust. Fascination. Jill was just some girl he'd felt sorry for in school, someone who didn't avoid his company or ignore him if he sat down next to her. If Vince loved her, he would have gone after her all those years ago.

But it would be nice to have what Sam and his wife, Annie, had...

As if anyone could love him.

Spinning on his heel, Vince shook off the romantic notion and barreled past the well-lit garage on his way to the shadowy driveway. He craved darkness, was nearly consumed with the need to disappear. Anything would be better than having to face Jill's continued rejection. He got enough of that from his grandfather.

As Vince passed into the gloom, someone bumped into his shoulder, sending his heart into overdrive. Vince reached out and grabbed hold. A pipe clattered onto the gravel drive, smoke rising from it in a big angry puff. Something small and white nipped and yapped at his ankles.

"Holy mackerel," Edda Mae said as Vince set her away from him. She was once more in her pink robe and slippers. "You grabbed me like a bear in heat."

"Looney!" Vince warned, bending to retrieve Edda Mae's pipe, his nostrils filling with tobacco smoke.

Moonbeam danced out of reach with a reproachful growl.

"Did you and Jill fight again?" Edda Mae took the pipe and knocked it against the garage wall. The smoldering tobacco fell to the ground.

Instead of answering, Vince ground the tobacco into the earth with his boot.

"I thought so. Come along then, boy." Edda Mae led the way back to her cottage.

Moonbeam followed, prancing sideways to keep one eye on Vince, who had no intention of tagging along. He needed to be alone. He drew one deep breath and then another, listening to the delicate click-click of the little dog's progress and the slower crunch of gravel beneath Edda Mae's feet.

"On a night like tonight with no moon you'll most likely twist your ankle heading down that hill." Edda Mae stood framed in the doorway to her cottage, welcoming light spilling out toward him. "Of course, it's your choice. Won't hurt my feelings none if you decline my offer."

The cold mountain wind taunted the branches above him. It really was too dark to go traipsing about. But if Vince went inside he'd have to act civilized.

"Well? Are you going to make me stand here all night?" she huffed.

"No," Vince grumbled. "But I'm not having any of your whiskey."

"Your loss. It's good medicine against bad dreams." She eyed him once before stepping into the cottage. "Not that you'd ever be plagued by those."

Vince wasn't in the mood to give anything away.

"Was it Teddy or the casino or both?" Edda Mae asked once she'd placed his steaming mug of coffee next to him and taken her seat with her mug of whiskey, Moonbeam on guard at her feet. "Won't hurt you none to tell me."

Vince took a sip of coffee, knowing it would burn his tongue. "Milch?" he choked out, his tongue rough against the roof of his mouth. It wasn't how he preferred his coffee, but it beat spilling his guts to Edda Mae.

She took his mug and disappeared into the kitchen. Moonbeam watched him with those beady little eyes of hers, lips twitching as if she was barely keeping herself from growling at him.

"I fixed it up real nice," Edda Mae said, trundling back out. "With milk and sugar. It's obvious you can't take the hard stuff. Must be the way they raise them in Nevada. Jill's the same."

Vince couldn't believe Jill liked her coffee diluted and sweet as candy. Vince dutifully took a sip of the tan concoction. Ugh. "This is perfect."

Edda Mae made a disappointed noise. "You're usually a better liar than that."

"Nobody lies about coffee." And to prove it Vince took another sip. But all the thick liquid did was coat his mouth and injure tongue. He set the mug down.

Edda Mae sat silently watching him. Moonbeam was still as a statue. A tree branch rubbed against the house. There was nothing to do but reach for the coffee again. Vince took another sip of the too-sweet brew, and then another when Edda Mae still stayed quiet. At a loss, Vince cradled the mug and returned her stare.

Edda Mae sighed and rubbed her wrist beneath the sleeve of her chenille robe. "I used to lie to myself when my husband was alive. And I kept things from him—little things, such as letting him think I had baked a cake when I had bought it. And big things, too. I kept myself from him, not opening my full heart, keeping secrets inside. I thought we'd have forever, but that wasn't to be, so I am left with…"

"Looney?" Vince supplied, trying to lighten the moment.

Edda Mae gave him her squinty-eyed gaze. "Part of knowing who you are is knowing what you want, and to do that you must be honest with yourself and others. A choice must be made. Since you don't like dogs, you could end up old and alone with just money for company. Is that what you want?"

Edda Mae's observations were a little too close to the mark. If Vince didn't negotiate a deal and his grandmother passed away, his grandfather would be on his own, surrounded only by people he paid to be there. Living by himself and denying his feelings was fine when Vince was twenty-eight, but he suddenly didn't want to be so much like his grandfather when he reached eighty. Perhaps it was the effect of the brief time he'd spent with Jill and Teddy, or perhaps this feeling had been there all along, lying dormant. Vince didn't know.

"You're in love with Jill," Edda Mae proclaimed.

"I'm not what she needs," Vince said, setting down the mug and standing, ignoring Moonbeam's warning woof. They had history, but he didn't love her. Jill was too fragile. If she couldn't face her own past, how could she possibly be strong enough to face his? Much less forgive him—for dishonoring their wedding vows, for being a coward on so many levels.

"You say this after one day spent arguing—"

"No." Restless from too much self-awareness, Vince headed for the door.

"Then you will continue down different paths," Edda Mae said sadly.

"You've got that right. We're getting a divorce." Vince left. He had to take care of Number One.

From this point forward, Jill is off-limits.

Jill's apartment was quiet and dark. She'd left a lamp on in the living room for him. His back spasmed at the thought of another night on Jill's short, lumpy couch.

Vince paced the floor, avoiding the kitchen. No one else knew Jill the way Vince did, no other man could get her to open up the way Vince could. But Jill wanted a divorce. Vince knew she'd find the right guy someday.

Keep your eye on the casino.

Only, the thought of another man possessing Jill angered him, caused him to wheel about aimlessly.

One thing was certain—he wasn't taking Teddy on that rafting trip. Jill wanted him out of her life and Teddy's. It was time he respected that and moved on, went to stay somewhere else. Maybe then he'd get his head straight.

What would he say to Teddy in the morning? He'd become fond of the little guy. Maybe Jill would let Teddy come visit him in Vegas.

On Vince's third lap around the room he noticed the permission form for the father-son rafting trip on the dining-room table. He grabbed the sheet and half crumpled it before he realized that Jill's signature graced the bottom.

Vince could have walked away from Jill in the morning, but he couldn't disappoint Teddy.

CHAPTER ELEVEN

WITH HER HIGH SCHOOL yearbook in her lap, Jill listened to Vince prowl around her home. She sat nestled in her dormer window, angling the book toward the citrus candle that lit the room on the small table to her left. The glossy pages held few memories for Jill. She hadn't been much of a joiner and neither had Vince. In his senior picture—with his tux, classic good looks and reserved smile—you couldn't tell much about him.

Photos of Craig were everywhere. He'd lettered in football, basketball and baseball. He'd been on the student council and had been crowned Homecoming King. Although Jill remembered him as an example of all-American wholesomeness, looking at Craig's pictures now, she saw something almost sad in his smile, as if he was just pretending to be happy for the camera.

Jill had always feared confronting Craig someday, knowing she'd be an emotional wreck. She'd played the scenario a thousand times in her mind. She'd stutter, her eyes would fill with tears and she'd have to run away before breaking down completely in front of the man who'd stolen her virginity. But tonight, gazing at Craig's young face and thinking about what Vince had told her, Jill felt none of the bitterness, none of the helplessness. She supposed she had Vince to thank for that. That was why she'd signed the form for Teddy, as a token of her appreciation, even as she hoped Teddy wouldn't be more enamored of Vince than ever after the rafting trip.

But she couldn't stay married to Vince. Oh, she'd like to stay married to him if she could go back to having an absentee husband and forget about the casino.

But she couldn't. She'd miss Vince when he was gone. She enjoyed sparring with him, relished his dimpled smile, cherished the warmth that crept into his eyes when he looked at her (and they weren't arguing).

Jill turned her attention back to Vince's senior picture. He had beautiful eyes—deep brown when he laughed, black when they kissed. Perhaps if they weren't pitted against each other on this casino, they could have enjoyed the friendship he seemed so intent on having with her.

Friends with benefits.

Jill's body tingled anew as she recalled Vince's chest pressed against hers, his mouth claiming hers. She'd be in control and they wouldn't even have to complete the deed. There were other ways to guarantee pleasure—hers and his. If only she could believe that Vince wouldn't go back on his word when things got too heated; if only he wasn't a shrewd businessman who couldn't be trusted.

After years of celibacy, years without looking at a guy with more than a fleeting moment of interest, Jill burned with longing for one man. The one man she shouldn't desire.

Her soon-to-be ex-husband.

"REMEMBER WHAT we practiced this morning," Vince coached Teddy as he adjusted the boy's life vest straps.

Dappled sunlight covered the narrow bank where pairs of dads and sons gathered. Most sported life vests over short-sleeved T-shirts. Vince wore a long-sleeved shirt beneath the vest he'd borrowed from Jill. Jimmy, Arnie's nephew, caught sight of Vince and gave him a tight nod, his scar defiantly on display.

Teddy grinned. "Pokémon is for babies. Spiderman may not be as strong as the others, but he's smarter than the rest."

"Good. And?"

Behind them several father-son pairs dragged their yellow inflatable rafts into the water with startled shouts at the mountain river's cold temperature.

"The Oakland Raiders rule football. Shaq kicks butt in the NBA, and…and the Yankees buy baseball championships from…China?"

"Japan. But that's close enough. High five, buddy. You're ready." Vince waved to Arnie when the other man caught his eye.

"Have you ever played cards?" Vince gestured for Teddy to pick up the other end of the raft.

"Go Fish?"

"Blackjack? Poker?" Teddy was such a quick study he'd be a natural.

"Nope." Teddy shrieked as one foot tested the frigid river. He backed up several steps, tugging the raft with him. "That's too cold."

"Yeah, well, you wanted to go." Vince glanced around at the other boys braving the water.

Teddy saw them, too, but he wasn't quite ready to

try again. "My grandma and grandpa own casinos. Mom says gambling makes money seem more important than it really is."

"Does she?"

Teddy shielded his eyes from the sun and looked at the first few rafts as they disappeared around the bend. "Don't say anything about gambling to Mom, okay?"

"Okay." He'd limit their arguments to casinos. "Now get your butt in that river."

JILL STOOD in front of the dining hall with Edda Mae after having buzzed the first of their guests through the gate. She missed Teddy by her side.

He'd been a live wire at the news that he was going rafting with Vince. It made Jill smile to remember the way he threw his skinny arms around her and yelled thank-you about a dozen times. On the other hand, she and Vince had hardly spoken.

"Where's Moonbeam?" Jill asked. Shady Oak seemed unnaturally quiet without Vince and Teddy.

"In my cottage."

Jill could see Moonbeam's little nose pressed against the front window. The dog liked to climb onto the top of Edda Mae's wing chair and look out. Thankfully, Moonbeam would only growl if someone came too close to her roost.

They both wore Shady Oak–emblazoned navy polo shirts and jeans that had seen better days as they watched a caravan of cars and SUVs fill the parking lot. They'd spent a hectic morning baking, rolling cutlery in napkins and going over the schedule— anything to help Jill prepare for a week without Edda

Mae. With the temperature in the midseventies and the sun only occasionally hiding behind the clouds, it was the perfect day for a drive in the mountains. Their guests should arrive in a good mood.

The credit-union managers stepped out onto the gravel in new blue jeans, twisting and stretching after their long drive. They hefted computer bags as they approached Jill and Edda Mae. Heaven forbid they should leave their equipment in the car. Out of habit, Jill counted twelve men. She squared her shoulders, feeling a newfound confidence.

"Welcome to Shady Oak. I'm Jill and this is Edda Mae." For once, Jill's smile didn't feel guarded. "We've got your room keys here and the dining hall set up for your afternoon meetings, complete with homemade cookies, coffee and soda."

"Fantastic. I'm Spencer Silva." A burly man with a shaved head stepped forward and shook Jill's hand. His belly hung over the waistband of his crisp jeans and his sneakers glowed with a brightness only new shoes could boast. He glanced at his watch and then turned back to the group. "We're right on schedule. We'll start in an hour."

"I have no signal."

"Me, neither."

Jill clung to her smile. The absence of a wireless signal sent some people into withdrawal. "You'll find your cell phones and PDAs won't work here. We're fifty miles away from the nearest transmission tower."

"I told you," Spencer said. "We're here to work—without interruption."

There was a definite restlessness in the crowd. Jill

promised every client that isolation was a team builder, not a cause for mutiny, but there was always this first moment of doubt.

"We're not completely in the Stone Age. We have DSL cables available in each of your rooms for computer hookup, as well as in the dining hall. There are phones in your room and there's a pay phone beneath the stairs to your left." Jill's cheeks were starting to hurt. "If you need to use your cell phone or PDA, you can drive into town and park at Railroad Stop's Museum and Pizza Parlor. That parking lot has been found to be the best location for receiving a signal." By her parents.

"Fantastic. I'm sure we won't need to take a drive just to check our messages." Spencer's tone made this more than a suggestion.

"Is there an Indian casino close by?" asked a blond man too young to be in a management position. He had startling blue eyes and a grin that had probably gotten him more than a job.

"No." Jill's smile slipped a notch. She almost expected to turn around and see Vince clapping because someone was supporting his agenda.

The sun slid behind a cloud.

"We have a full schedule," Spencer said. "No time for excursions."

"But if we wanted to go in the evening, how far would we need to drive?" A few more years in the corporate world and the blond probably wouldn't be so persistent.

"Henderson." Spencer frowned in warning.

Or maybe young Henderson was just a pain in the ass who'd never learn, never change and never be promoted. Jill sent up a silent apology to Henderson's mother and then gathered all her patience as she prepared to deal with the issue.

"The nearest casino is down in Jackson. Fifty miles of winding road there and another fifty back," Edda Mae piped up before Jill could speak. "The Highway Patrol like to sit on the outskirts of Jackson and ticket drinkers, and the ones they don't get sometimes end up in the ditch at Dead Man's Curve."

Henderson smiled at Edda Mae. "You're pulling my leg."

"*Pah.* Wouldn't disrespect you like that. We've only just met. But you look barely old enough to vote, much less gamble."

The group laughed, including Henderson, and the tension dissipated, but Jill couldn't help but recall Vince saying that her business would benefit from a casino.

"COME ON, TEDDY," Pete, a roly-poly boy with a freckle-faced grin, shouted over his shoulder as he ran back toward the water. "Let's skip rocks."

"Can I?" Teddy bit his lip and turned to Vince as if he needed his permission.

"Of course," Vince said, an odd feeling blossoming in his chest as he watched Teddy race after his new friend. *So this was what it felt like to be a dad. A good dad.* He couldn't wait to tell somebody about it. Vince felt important, as if he'd somehow managed entry into an exclusive club he'd been banned from for a long time. It made his soggy clothing and aching muscles much easier to bear.

They were at a picnic area on a slow bend in the

Mokelumne River. Arnie was working with some of the other dads to start a fire in the fire pit. Vince had been told they were going to cook all their food over an open flame. A meal of blackened hot dogs and melted marshmallows wasn't gourmet, but it wasn't something Vince had ever experienced, either.

He smiled as he surveyed the boisterous group. Several dads were comparing stories about going over the dwindling, rocky rapids so late in the season. Some of the older guys grimaced and moved stiffly, when they moved at all.

Some of the older boys were tossing a Frisbee near the water's edge. And then Vince's gaze fell on Jimmy, sitting by himself and drinking a soda at a picnic table not far from where Vince stood.

"If you want to look so bad, here." Jimmy thrust his arm toward Vince.

"I'm not staring."

Jimmy huffed, clearly not believing him. "What you see is scar tissue. What I see is my sister right before my father killed her."

Oh, God. It made Vince's scar seem like a scratch in comparison. Without taking his eyes from Jimmy's, Vince approached him. "How old?"

"She was seven." The words came out on a hoarse whisper despite the I-don't-care curl to Jimmy's lip.

"No. How old were you?"

"Ten," Jimmy admitted mulishly, running a hand over the puckered skin on his arm.

Vince stopped a few feet from Jimmy's bench. "You must have been very brave."

"She died," he retorted.

"I was twenty-five, serving my first tour in Iraq, when a bullet tore through my arm." Vince resisted the urge to roll up his sleeve, clamped down on the memory of gunfire and the way he'd frozen, becoming an easy target. This wasn't a game of who had the more gruesome injury or the more brutal recollections. "I look at your arm—at *you*—because I admire your courage. The fact that you don't hide your scar…" Or his painful past. "That makes you a man in my eyes."

Jimmy studied Vince's long sleeves with curiosity and a grudging respect Vince didn't feel he deserved. And he knew his bare arm would never see the light of day again.

"Hey, Jimmy!"

"Jim-mee, come play Frisbee."

With a curt nod, Jimmy rejoined his friends, looking back only once.

"DID YOU HAVE FUN?" Jill asked when the apartment door opened around nine-thirty Sunday night. Her guests were safely tucked up in their cottages after several productive hours of meetings and an abundance of good food and wine. She'd heard no more grumbling about the absence of cell-phone service or nearby casinos.

Teddy rushed over and gave Jill a hit-and-run hug before falling onto the couch. "It was awesome."

Vince came in, walking like John Wayne.

"Everybody loved Vince. He makes the best weenie on a stick—it's mostly black and crispy. There's a trick to it. He taught me so the next time our guests have a bonfire I can roast weenies for them." Teddy paused for breath. "Only I need to get just the right stick. You'll help me find one, won't you, Vince?"

"Sure." Vince stopped to lean over a chair as if he was in desperate need of support.

"What happened to you?" Jill would not feel sympathy for Vince.

"We went over the rapids," Vince grumbled.

"That's what you do when you go rafting," Jill pointed out, trying not to smile.

"Teddy started to bounce a little too much and I—"

"I almost fell out of the raft. Vince saved me." Teddy rolled over on the couch, still on a natural high. He stared at the ceiling, no doubt reliving some thrill from earlier in the day. "It was so cool."

Jill swore her heart stopped beating. She never should have let Vince take Teddy. Vince didn't have enough experience on the river. She was halfway to Teddy before she realized she'd moved.

"There's not a scratch on *him*. I ended up on the bottom of the raft with Teddy in my lap," Vince explained.

"And we hit a ton of rocks," Teddy filled in. "Again and again and again. Water went everywhere."

Jill took in the way Vince was standing, his stance too wide, a death grip on the chair back. "Do you need an ice pack?"

"For his butt?" Teddy dissolved into giggles.

"Aspirin, then." Jill took pity on Vince. After all, he'd saved her baby. "If you were so sore, how come you didn't come home earlier?"

"I was fine standing around the campfire. I didn't

stiffen up until we drove back." They'd taken Edda Mae's truck, which had old, worn-out shocks, so every bump must have been murder on his backside.

"I can't wait until next year." Teddy practically ran into the kitchen after Jill. "Mom, I want to visit Vince in Las Vegas. Can I?"

"No."

"But Vince says they have paintings there." His eyes glowed. He'd loved painting since he'd first finger-painted at age two.

"The Sicilian has quite a collection, including a Picasso in my grandfather's private quarters," Vince said.

Vince wasn't helping. "Occupy your mouth with these." Jill gave Vince two aspirin and a glass of water.

"Please, Mom."

"Teddy, I'm not going to make promises I can't keep." Vince was bound to disappear permanently from their lives now that she was divorcing him. And if his casino deal went through, he'd only be in town a day or so each year—not enough time to establish a meaningful relationship with Teddy.

"But, Mom—"

"Ixnay on the eggingbay," Vince whispered.

"As if I don't know pig Latin." Jill narrowed her eyes at Vince. "What else did you teach him?"

"Only how to make friends and be cool." Teddy collapsed back on the couch. "I love having a dad."

She'd been right. Vince was ruining her son. He'd never be happy having a single parent again.

"Teddy, you have school tomorrow. Go get ready for bed."

The day, which had ended so successfully for Jill's business, was now sour and bleak.

VINCE WAS MISERABLE. He lay like a pretzel on his stomach on Jill's couch. It had been a hot day and Jill's apartment was stuffy. Vince had taken his shirt off and tried for what must have been the hundredth time to fall asleep. But he couldn't ignore his body's aches, couldn't stop second-guessing decisions and recalling feelings he'd had in the past about Jill, or keep from playing out scenarios for the casino deal. Vince didn't love Jill, but he'd decided on a course of action and he was going to stick to it. Maybe Jill would come to her senses and maybe she wouldn't.

Light flooded the room and Vince squinted.

"You need a hit of Edda Mae's whiskey." Jill walked past the couch. She wore a tank top and soft flannel pajama bottoms that clung to the curve of her hips. "Your thrashing makes it hard for anyone to sleep."

Vince reached out as she passed. He'd always gone after what he wanted. His bare arm and empty hand dangled over the couch.

His scar. Trying to tug his shirt back on while lying down sent Vince tumbling off the couch. After the day he'd had Vince decided to stay on the floor. It made it that much easier for Jill to walk all over him. "You could have given me a little warning."

"Gee, like you gave me when you showed up at the town meeting?" Jill's voice drifted out from the kitchen.

"I was busy. I meant to call," Vince grumbled. He just hadn't worked up the nerve.

"Or when you blindsided me with the rafting trip?"

"That was a spur-of-the-moment thing."

"Or how about—"

"Enough! I get the picture. *Wife* wants more communication."

"Wife?"

"Like it or not, that's what you are," Vince mumbled into the carpet. She'd seen his arm.

"We never even…you know. It's like a nonbinding, unfulfilled—"

"Oh, hell, no. You either wear the ring or you don't."

"Which would explain your string of so-called one-nighters as…" Jill knelt next to him.

"A desperate cry for attention from my wife during a long and painful separation?"

"Proof you don't think of yourself as married?" Jill helped Vince up off the floor.

The feel of her hands on him nearly made Vince weep, but he was in no condition to sweet-talk her into touching him some more. Every muscle protested, every joint ached. "If that were true I would have a long-term live-in girlfriend."

Jill hesitated before pressing a shot glass into his hands, confirmation that his words gave her pause. And why didn't he have a live-in girlfriend? Why had he spent the past ten years of his life making mistakes—with her, his grandfather, his career. The list went on.

"Edda Mae's home brew?" he asked, trying to grin, desperate to elicit a smile from Jill.

"Looney Mooneyshine?" Jill said, straight-faced.

"That sounds like something Teddy would come up with."

They stared at each other for a moment. Jill was probably just as tense as he was and unable to relax enough to laugh.

"You aren't joining me, *wife?*" he asked when he couldn't take her silence anymore.

"I've got to get up early and make breakfast for the guests."

"Chicken."

Jill stepped back, not taking the bait.

Vince examined the clear liquid from several angles before downing it in one gulp. Immediately, his esophagus flamed with heat and he struggled for air. The room spun.

Jill pounded his back until Vince gasped enough air to fill his lungs. "Are you crazy? That stuff could kill a horse." Holding his head, Vince dropped onto the couch.

She plunked herself down on a chair next to him. "Tell me about your scar, the one on your arm."

"I thought you were going to bed."

"I've decided I've told you far too much about me. It's time to even the score." Was she trying not to smile? Vince couldn't tell.

With surprisingly steady fingers, Vince set the shot glass on the coffee table, resisting the urge to tug down his shirtsleeves further. "I'm not drunk enough."

"Would you tell me if you had another?"

God, he hoped not.

"It looks like a nasty bullet wound." Jill gave Vince a clinical once-over and he felt a totally different kind of heat, one she probably hadn't meant to create.

"Did you get it in the war?"

"Go to bed, *wife.*" And now Vince's mind conjured

up a different picture. Jill in bed, beckoning him to join her. He'd seen her green-and-white quilt, could imagine her on it, naked and crooking her finger at him.

"Not yet," she said.

Edda Mae's whiskey was trouble. Warmth spread to Vince's fingertips. He glanced at Jill, at the generous swell of her breasts, at the nipples pressing against the thin yellow material of her tank top.

He curled his hands into fists. "Go on. Unless you want to trade secrets like—" he nearly said *lovers* "—schoolgirls, you better leave."

Jill shifted, glanced at Vince's right arm and then away.

Silence hung between them, increasingly leaden with every heartbeat, until Vince was sure nothing could break it.

"It's all about control, isn't it?" Jill said with a sigh. "Your scar. My past."

Vince shook his head. "It's not about control. It's about self-preservation."

"He made me feel helpless." Jill's words fell between them almost like a whimper, an acknowledgment of her pain. "You know my wounds. I think it's only fair I know about yours."

Vince was reminded of Jimmy, flaunting his pain for everyone to see. Vince had it all wrong. Jill was strong enough to deal with his scars. It was Vince who didn't want to share them, who wasn't brave enough to bare his soul to her.

"Good night, *wife*." Vince needed to push Jill away, to cover his head with a pillow and hide.

"But—"

"If you stay and I show you my scar—" that hideous reminder of his near disastrous failure "—there's a cost," Vince warned as he raised his eyes and let Jill see the burning need there. "The next woman to see my scar will be my wife in every way."

It was nonnegotiable. Vince had to possess Jill. The power of it scared him. He was no better than Craig.

"You don't mean that," Jill whispered.

Vince let his expression speak for him and before he knew it, he was alone.

CHAPTER TWELVE

"YOU'RE UP EARLY," Edda Mae noted as she made her way to the coffeepot the next morning. "Even for you."

Jill had bacon sizzling in a pan and four dozen eggs whipped up and ready to scramble. There was too much on her mind: Vince and his scar, Teddy's longing for a father, Vince's kiss, not to mention the day's chores at Shady Oak. Jill had tossed and turned all night and eventually called it quits around five a.m. "Can you slice the bagels and set out the muffins?"

"Just let me get a shot of go-go juice first." Edda Mae filled a mug with steaming black coffee. "How did the rafting trip go?"

"They had a great time."

"You did the right thing."

"Did I? Teddy wants to visit Vince in Vegas." Jill didn't mention that Teddy also wanted Vince as his dad, while Vince had kept silent on the subject.

"Teddy's not a baby anymore, Jill. It's time to let him test his wings," Edda Mae said, setting her coffee cup down by the bag of bagels.

"He's only ten and unfortunately for him, he'll always be my baby. Did you open the gate? I'm expecting a delivery."

Edda Mae nodded. "This situation with Vince and Teddy reminds me of a story—"

"No time for stories, not if you're going to Francie's today," Jill cut her off as gently as she could.

"I feel better about going with Vince here. He can't be so busy with Arnie that he won't find time to help you in the kitchen. I forgot to ask if he's a good cook."

"He's leaving this morning."

"That's what you said yesterday."

But today was different. Jill wasn't sleeping with Vince and there was no way she was supporting his casino. Jill would turn down any deal Vince offered.

"Watch out, Jill. You're burning the bacon," Edda Mae said.

Jill began quickly scooping bacon strips out of the frying pan.

The trouble was, you could pay attention and still have everything you'd dreamed about and worked for go up in smoke.

"COME ON, VINCE. You take longer to get ready than Mom." Teddy danced at the bathroom door, watching Vince shave.

"What's your hurry?" Vince deadpanned. "Do we have time for another joke?"

"No."

The kid was bouncing off the walls with uncontained excitement. He'd been telling jokes as if no one had ever listened to him before. Vince was still stiff and sore from the rafting trip, although Edda Mae's whiskey had helped him sleep.

"I have to eat breakfast and get to the bus stop,"

Teddy babbled. "Why are you so slow? I thought grownups were always busy. Don't you have work to do?"

"Yes. I have a meeting." Gone were the jeans and western shirt. Vince was expecting Arnie this morning, so he'd put on fine wool slacks, a white button-down shirt and a tie.

"About what?"

"About a casino I want to build in town." Arnie was going to show Vince the blueprints. Vince couldn't help being eager.

"Oh." The excitement burst out of Teddy like a popped balloon. He stopped moving. "I forgot. We don't want one of those."

"It's not such a bad thing." Vince stuffed his razor back into his shaving kit.

Teddy shook his head slowly, his gaze so solemn that Vince's heart filled with doubt. And then Teddy whispered, "If you build the casino, will you still be my stepdad?"

God, I hope so. But he couldn't promise anything, except, "I'll always be something to you, at the very least, a friend."

Teddy rolled his eyes. "I hope not. I've got enough friends. Come on, I have a surprise for Mom." And then Teddy loped down the hall. "Last one downstairs has stinky feet!"

Realizing after one quick step his bruised and battered body couldn't move as fast as Teddy's, Vince accepted his smelly status and went down the stairs like his grandfather.

"Mom, don't move. There's a spider on you," Teddy said from behind Jill a few minutes later when Vince walked in. He put his forefinger to his lips and grinned at Vince who stood in the doorway to the large kitchen.

"Where? Teddy, get it off." Jill's voice shook, but she stood very still, clearly frightened, one hand frozen on a frying pan full of scrambled eggs.

With playful wickedness, Teddy's fingers danced across the collar of Jill's shirt. Her entire body started to shake.

Vince frowned from where he stood by the doorway. "Teddy—"

"Get it off! Get it off!" Jill started a panicky version of the Snoopy dance. Her feet were moving, but she wasn't going anywhere.

Teddy was laughing silently, his fingers still freaking Jill out.

"Is it off? Is it off me?" Jill suddenly flinched away as if this might get rid of the spider. Scrambled eggs flew everywhere. Jill stopped moving, glanced back at Teddy's hand still raised in the air and at the eggs on the floor, the cupboards, her sneakers. *"Teddy!"*

"What's going on in there?" Edda Mae called from the dining room. She'd been setting up an easel with a fresh pad of flip-chart paper.

"Nothing we can't handle," Jill said, glowering at Teddy.

Consumed with laughter, Teddy collapsed against Vince. "Wasn't that cool?"

"No. It was thoughtless and stupid and…" Vince became aware of how pale Teddy's upturned face had become. "It wasn't cool."

"I thought you liked me," Teddy said, looking up at Vince with tearful eyes.

Jill set down the frying pan with a clatter. "Teddy, you can have cold breakfast this morning. Upstairs. Alone."

Vince couldn't look away from Teddy's disappointed expression, couldn't shake the feeling that he'd ruined their relationship.

"She needed to laugh," Teddy spoke barely above a whisper.

"Now, Teddy." There was something dictatorial in Jill's voice that had Vince wanting to march upstairs with him.

"Grown-ups are so lame," Teddy tossed over his shoulder before disappearing out the door. He'd said grown-ups, but Vince knew he meant one grown-up in particular.

Vince listened to Teddy's footsteps pounding up the stairs, cringed slightly when the door slammed and then turned to Jill. "What just happened? He hates me."

"He doesn't hate you. You did the right thing," Jill said, swabbing up the mess at his feet. "Welcome to parenthood. It stings at first, but you get used to it."

"One minute we were joking and the next he was out of control."

"He knows I hate spiders. I woke up once with one trying to crawl up my nose, and he's taken advantage ever since." Jill tossed the last paper towel full of eggs into the trash and got out the mop and pail from a nearby closet. "Boys have a different sense of humor than girls."

Needing something to do other than stare at Jill, Vince filled a mug with coffee. "I don't remember."

Jill whisked the mop around without glancing up, suddenly more like the demure, unsure girl of his school days. "That's because you weren't a normal boy."

He'd already admitted as much, but Vince didn't like Jill saying it.

"You probably never pulled a prank on your mother," Jill went on as if unaware she'd just hit a soft spot.

Considering his mother was a high-maintenance, high-strung former showgirl, Vince had to agree, but still—

"And you didn't hang out with the other boys, which probably explains why now you look like you stepped out of *GQ* magazine every day."

"I didn't hang out with *anyone*." The older Vince had gotten, the less accepting the cliquish private-school students were of a boy who had too much hurt and anger bottled up inside. "And lay off my work clothes."

But Jill was on a roll now and paid no attention to his words. "So it makes perfect sense that you'd never put a frog in your mom's mop bucket." Jill leaned down to examine her handiwork. With a satisfied nod, she put the mop and pail back in the cupboard and then washed her hands. "Or try to use your mom's bra as a slingshot."

Now there was an image that got Vince's attention, making him wonder how softly stretchy his wife's bra might be. Accommodating enough for his hand?

As if sensing the degenerate nature of his thoughts, Jill's cheeks flushed and she busied herself with fixing more eggs.

This conversation was loaded with more pitfalls than a blind date. Sexual attraction was the least of his worries. Unfortunately it was the most pressing of them.

"Are you saying," Vince began when he'd had a few more moments to pull himself together and decipher her speech, "that Teddy misbehaves when he's with other boys? Or with me?"

"Well, kids need limits. The adult sets the example. Teddy's starting to push you now, to see how far you'll let him go."

"Great."

"Parenting isn't all fun and games, not in the long haul." She scrutinized him.

Vince suspected she was about to ask if he was up to the task, but there was a knock on the kitchen door.

"That'll be our grocery delivery." But when Jill opened the door Arnie stood there. His slow perusal of her body had Jill wanting to back up a step, but she held her ground, curling her hand into a fist behind her back. "What do you want?"

"Good morning to you, too. Is your husband home?"

Jill hesitated.

And then Vince's arm was around Jill's shoulders, his lips pressing a gentle kiss to her temple. Jill didn't know whether to melt against Vince in relief or stomp his foot.

"Sweetheart, I forgot to tell you Arnie was dropping by this morning."

"Have I come at a bad time?"

Yes. "No." If glares were daggers, Jill would have pinned Arnie against the porch railing. If Jill had more nerve Vince would be next to Arnie with a well-placed knife just below his crotch.

How could he invite Arnie up here?

"Arnie, why don't you wait for me out back?" Vince said. "You can go through the double doors to your right." He still held Jill in the crook of his arm. "I'll bring coffee."

"Sure." But Arnie didn't move.

After a moment Vince turned Jill to face him, cradled her face in his hands and kissed her lightly on the lips. *"Wife."* Vince pulled back and shut the door.

Jill knew the kiss was for Arnie's benefit, but that didn't mean her heart didn't race at Vince's touch or his teasing endearment.

"Don't worry about Arnie," he said.

"It's none of your concern," Jill managed to say. And it wasn't. Arnie would leave Jill alone once the casino project went forward or died.

"I'll fix it," Vince sighed, letting her go.

"You'll do no such thing," she hissed at him. "I'm divorcing you."

"But until we've both signed away our marriage, *you're mine.*" Vince's black eyes burned with anger. "And he's going to know it."

Jill gripped the counter when Vince said *you're mine.* "You said I had to prove I could stand on my own."

"I lied," he said through gritted teeth.

"Well, if it's so important to you, why don't you step outside and punch Arnie in the nose? You'd get what you want—satisfying a Neanderthal urge to draw blood—and so would I. No more casino." It was unlikely Arnie would put up with such humiliation.

"I hate it when you think you're right," Vince said, considering her.

Jill smiled in triumph, fully expecting him to scowl at her.

Instead, Vince grinned right back, flashing her those perfect teeth and annoying dimple as he stroked her nose with one finger. "I'll punch him after we ink the deal."

Jill threw the dish towel at his back. But really, how hurtful was a dish towel?

"HOPE YOU LIKE your coffee black," Vince said, handing Arnie a mug, but in his mind's eye he was tossing the mug to the ground and taking a swing at the older man. Funny thing was, Vince was just as calculating as Arnie, especially when it came to Jill. What right did Vince have to stake any claim other than a paper marriage?

Arnie balanced the mug on the porch railing while holding a rolled-up set of papers. "Nice view out here. I tried to get Edda Mae to sell this property to the tribe and get involved in the casino, but she had other ideas."

It was Vince's wife who had the ideas, but Vince wasn't getting into a pissing match. Jill was right. Vince had to keep his temper. But the anger felt good because it bolstered the decision he'd made about the deal.

Vince frowned. He'd never let consequences influence his business decisions before, yet this time something constantly nagged his conscience.

As if sensing Vince's tension, Arnie tossed Vince a sideways glance. "Did I come at a bad time?" he repeated.

"Are those the plans?" Vince asked, more than ready to get this meeting over with.

"Yes." Arnie unrolled them against the railing. "The architect did a fabulous job capturing the Indian-lodge feeling on the outside."

Sure enough, the front looked as if it was made of logs, and it had a tall portico so that guests could drive up to the front door and request valet parking, even in their RVs. The "logs" were huge, perhaps eight to ten feet around, and looked real, instead of formed from plaster.

Vince kept his voice even. "What about wear and tear? Plaster chips easily."

"We've budgeted for a newer compound. It's tougher. They use it in all the amusement parks now."

With a nod Vince flipped to the next page, which detailed the casino interior—a manmade brook, lined with trees and crossed by foot bridges, wound its way through the main floor. Vince counted the slot machines, the blackjack and crap tables. State law allowed a minimum of each and they had been drawn to scale.

Vince turned to the page that depicted the bar.

"It has a Western saloon feel with just enough elegant touches to keep it from being clichéd," Arnie said, a note of pride in his voice. "Each side of the bar has a different theme, one for each of the traditional stories told by the Native Americans in the area." Arnie continued explaining his vision while Vince calculated costs and revenue in his head.

The design was classy yet not overly ambitious. It would complement Shady Oak perfectly.

"What's this?" Vince pointed to a substantial amount of space.

"It's our, um, keno lounge. The stage area is just behind it."

Vince peered at the crossed-out label. "It says 'storyteller stage.' And 'dancers dressing room.'"

"Like I said, Edda Mae turned us down." Arnie lasted about five more seconds before cracking under Vince's hard stare. "We assumed she'd want her storytelling to benefit the tribe. Jill obviously had other plans."

"You were going to have dancers on stage with Edda Mae?" Vince visualized Edda Mae in traditional Native American costume and topless dancers behind her.

Arnie shrugged. "Edda Mae has been our tribe's storyteller for years. I thought we could do something tasteful like they do at Hawaiian luaus with all the dancers fully clothed. We wouldn't need to book lounge acts if Edda Mae agreed to work with us."

Since it sounded like something his grandfather would do, Vince could understand the idea, but that didn't mean he was going to put up with Arnie hounding Jill or Edda Mae. "It's not going to happen. Tell me about your permits."

"The paperwork is filled out and waiting funding approval." Arnie nodded. "I estimated a year for construction."

A year? There's where the overconfidence of the amateur came in. The tribe could never pull off a job like this in a year. Such bravado meant weakness. Arnie had played right into Vince's hands. Vince named the amount, totaling several millions, he was willing to put up for the project—Arnie's eyes lit up— and then Vince told him the percentage of the profits he'd want his grandfather's company to receive— Arnie's expression sobered.

"That's more than we budgeted," Arnie said. "I'm counting on the casino to help my people. That leaves us barely enough to pave the roads in and out of town. It'll make it hard to garner the support of local businesses."

"You're asking me to invest without any up-front incentives. You've got to give me something." Vince laughed, but it was a hollow sound. It was too much to hope that Arnie would turn down such a lucrative offer. "Besides, the jobs created will help supplement improvements in the community through increased taxes, just like you said."

"I'll have to run this by the tribal council." Arnie clenched his jaw.

"Of course."

"They may not buy it." Arnie tried once more to pressure Vince.

Vince shrugged. "Just in case they do, I'll have my lawyers draw up the contracts. You'll have them by the end of the week."

"You know," Arnie said, rolling up the plans, "we'll be needing a CEO."

"I assumed that would be you."

"We'd benefit from hiring someone with casino-management experience. Someone with a local, vested interest...." Arnie raised his eyebrows and glanced back toward the kitchen.

"Me?" Vince laughed. "I'm a Vegas boy, bright lights, big city, lots of action. Railroad Stop is..." Vince searched for the right word. It was sleepy and exciting, laid back and fast-paced, welcoming and annoying—the contrasts all provided by Jill and Teddy. But he couldn't imagine living here year-round, owning a four-wheel drive that you actually needed, going without cell service and not wearing a shirt and tie to keep people at a distance.

"It never hurts to ask," Arnie said when Vince couldn't complete his sentence. "I wasn't sure if you'd be staying or not. I'll look for those contracts, but don't be surprised if we don't sign."

So they'd counter-offer. That was normal. This feeling that Arnie was poaching on Vince's turf was not. "You know, Arnie, Jill and I have been married a long time."

"And yet you didn't know she was the mayor." Arnie tapped the rolled-up plans back against his palm. "I have a feeling that things are going to change around here."

"Not everything." Vince flexed his fingers on his coffee cup.

Arnie laughed. "Jill's in over her head. And with you leaving…"

"Jill doesn't like you," Vince said coldly. "And the moment your casino begins to become a reality, she'll hate your guts."

"Jill's going to need someone in Railroad Stop, someone who's patient enough to outlast her tantrums and bad decisions, someone local who's willing to take on a package deal."

Vince would have bet serious money that Arnie's ideal package consisted of Jill and Shady Oak, not Jill and Teddy. Vince struggled to keep his voice even. "She's my *wife*. Stay away from her if you want this deal to go through."

"Funny." Arnie gave Vince a speculative look. "You haven't warned me off because you love her."

The problem was, Vince cared too much for Jill to let her fall in love with him.

Vince turned away before he threw a punch he wasn't sure he'd regret. As Arnie left the porch, Vince drew his BlackBerry from his belt clip and typed out an e-mail to his grandfather and their lawyer with the project details. With the offer made, Vince could return home and leave the negotiations to someone else.

When Vince pressed the "send" button, he got the hourglass icon. No signal. Of course.

Vince considered running upstairs to use Jill's landline, but Teddy was still there pouting. There was plenty of time later to send the message.

WHILE EDDA MAE finished her packing, Jill went into the dining hall with a tray to bus tables. She was surprised to see Arnie mingling with her guests, the word *casino* drifting to her ears as he munched on a piece of bacon.

"I think it would be fun to come up here and be able to gamble in the evenings. There's only so much peace and quiet a guy can take." It was Mr. I-Think-I'm-a-Blond-Stud doing the head bob with Arnie.

"Gambling is a great team-building exercise," another guest piped in, too cheerful by far. "The team that loses together all shows up to work the next morning."

Everyone had a hearty chuckle at that one.

"Can I help you?" Jill knew Arnie would recognize her smile to be one hundred percent phony. She wanted to pinch his ear and drag him out of the dining hall.

"Jill, may I have a moment?" Arnie made to take Jill's arm, but she'd had years to learn men's tricks, so she saw it coming and danced ahead of him toward the kitchen.

Jill waited for the door to swing closed behind Arnie, keeping the tray in front of her chest like a shield. "I'm not running a coffee shop. You can't just drop in here and talk to my guests."

Arnie held up his hands. "I'm sorry. A man gets pretty desperate when a deal is about to slip through his fingers."

He was up to something, but Jill just wasn't sure what.

"You've done a fantastic job out here, Jill. Our businesses could have complemented each other."

Could have? Jill looked out the pass-through to the dining-room windows, but the porch was empty. Vince wouldn't have backed out, not when he wanted so badly to patch up his relationship with his grandfather.

Arnie smiled ruefully as he made his way out the door, leaving Jill to wonder if Vince had changed his mind. Had she convinced Vince to bail?

CHAPTER THIRTEEN

"AND SO ALL THE ANIMALS copied each other and the hunters who came upon them were confused." Edda Mae stood before the fireplace in the dining room. "Owls purring? Panthers hooting? Snakes squeaking? The hunters didn't know which animals were friends and which to kill for food."

Vince had come back to the kitchen after packing his few things. His job in Railroad Stop was done. He needed to hit the road. So why was he dragging his feet?

"This is the best part." Teddy sidled next to Vince and slipped his small hand into Vince's larger one, the morning's drama forgotten.

This was why. Teddy had carved a spot for himself in a corner of Vince's heart, right next to Jill.

"So the hunters killed them all," Edda Mae said. "Every one of those animals died because they were too scared to be who they really were. And that is the story of Animal Envy."

The room was hushed for several seconds and then the audience broke out in applause. Edda Mae waved once before exiting through the back door.

Jill stood at the fireplace. Her hair was down, framing her face. She looked confident in her blue jeans and untucked polo shirt with the Shady Oak logo. "As you plan the rest of your day," she said, "I hope you'll have time to get some fresh air. There's a trail that leads to a bluff with a fantastic view, a place considered by local Native American tribes to be holy ground. It takes about forty-five minutes to walk there. Later this morning I'll be bringing you fresh coffee and coffee cake. Lunch is promptly at noon. Have a good meeting." Jill turned the floor over to one of her guests, looking as if she was exactly where she wanted to be.

Vince drew a deep breath. He'd come to Railroad Stop hoping everything would fall easily into place. He'd known what he had to do and, more importantly, who he was supposed to be. He wasn't sure about anything anymore.

"Where's everybody gone?" he asked Jill. Teddy had disappeared, along with Edda Mae.

"Edda Mae's going to drop Teddy off at school on her way to Fresno."

Now would be the perfect time to tell Jill he was leaving, too.

Jill's gaze bounced around the kitchen. "I need to say goodbye to Edda Mae and get started on the cottages." But she didn't leave and Vince said nothing.

And Vince did have something to say. He wanted to tell Jill that he was recommending his grandfather finance Arnie's casino.

Instead, he found himself outside, struggling to find a way to say goodbye to Teddy that didn't sound too sappy or too cold.

"You know we're friends, right?" Vince hooked his fingers onto the lip of the open truck window where

Teddy sat. *Friends.* Part of him wanted so much more than that. But what right did he have? He hadn't given Teddy life, just his name. "I have to leave today."

Chin thrust out, eyes straight ahead, Teddy nodded once.

"Here's my number. You can call me anytime." When Teddy didn't take Vince's business card, Vince laid it on the dashboard to the tune of Moonbeam's rumbling growl. "Spiderman forever, dude." Disregarding Moonbeam's displeasure from her spot in the middle of the bench seat, Vince held out his fist, ready to bang it against Teddy's, but Teddy's hands remained clasped in his lap.

"You think about what I said the other night," Edda Mae said, her gaze piercing.

After a curt nod from Vince, Edda Mae put the truck in gear. Vince watched them roll down the gravel driveway, perhaps imagining that Teddy's eyes caught his in the side-view mirror, one flash of blue before the boy disappeared down the hill with Edda Mae.

The pressure was off. He should feel relieved. Arnie had handed him a perfect set of plans and a deal that could help people in Railroad Stop, including Jill, if she'd only see it. His grandfather would be pleased with the terms.

Jill would be crushed.

The click of the door to his left told him that Jill had gone inside, probably to check on her guests. He looked up at the sky, but it wasn't the clear blue it had been the past two days. Instead, low gray clouds hung above the trees. He had no more reason to stay.

Vince entered the kitchen. "I need to tell you something."

"You're leaving," Jill said calmly.

Maybe Jill saw in his eyes some of the panic and urgency he was feeling. Maybe she just thought he was talking too loud and her guests might hear him. Maybe she needed to hold his hand as much as he wanted to hold hers. Whatever the reason, Jill took Vince by the hand and led him outside. But she didn't let go once the door closed behind them. She continued to tug him gently along and he followed as docile as a lap dog.

Jill stopped at a boulder on the trail they'd taken the other morning when he'd first kissed her. With both hands, Jill gently urged Vince to sit down and then pinned him with her bright blue gaze as she sat on a smaller rock at his feet. Vince opened his mouth to explain to Jill why he was leaving, but nothing came out.

"Why don't you tell me how you got this?" Jill touched Vince's right sleeve.

"It's nothing."

She shrugged. "If that's the case, you won't mind talking about it. You won't mind showing—"

As Jill reached for his wrist, Vince jerked away. "No."

"Edda Mae says Shady Oak is about finding the truth, forging a new path."

"Save it for a bunch of credit-union managers," Vince scoffed.

"Some people like to get away. Clear the air. Make some space. Figure things out without a lot of background noise."

"I get the picture, *wife*."

"I'm not sure you do," she murmured.

They stared at each other. Vince imagined his expression was just as stubborn as hers.

Finally Jill's face fell in disappointment. "This path leads to the top of the mountain. Sacred ground. Edda Mae says you can shout your anger at the world up there and only the gods will hear you. Take a walk past cabin number nine. You might find what you're looking for, if you're ready to face the truth." With a shrug, Jill turned to go.

Vince raised a hand to stop Jill as she walked away, but she was out of reach and he had no truths to tell. And yet he couldn't let Jill leave him. "Wait."

She hesitated.

"The things you want to know about me, the things you deserve to know about your husband...they aren't pretty." And could turn Jill against him forever.

"If you're concerned with appearing perfect, you don't understand anything."

"I understand how the world works and how others see me," Vince whispered as he watched Jill walk away.

HE'S NOT MY RESPONSIBILITY.

If he wanted to jump at every loud noise, far be it from Jill to stand in his way. She just thought if he talked about it, he'd feel better. Vince was just too stubborn.

He's not my responsibility.

Jill had cleaned rooms all morning, repeating the litany in her head. Now as she prepared a deli tray, sliced rolls and tossed a salad, as she slid a tray of brownies into the oven, she was still trying to convince herself. Vince wasn't her husband, not in the ways that counted. They had nothing in common. He was scheming and self-centered.

But he'd helped her let go of the past, of the bitterness that Craig had marked her with. Oh, it wasn't all gone. Jill was still jittery when men came too close or when Arnie acted like he could control her with sexual innuendo. But she'd kissed Vince, not once but twice.

And she wanted to kiss him again.

That wasn't quite right. She wanted to take Vince up on the offer he'd made Saturday night. Who else would she be able to feel safe having almost-sex with? The more she thought about it, the more she trusted Vince to back down if she asked him to.

Why shouldn't she use Vince when he'd tried to use her?

Because it wasn't fair to either of them to get that close without knowing each other's secrets. Sex was scary. Making love was…not so much. But she wasn't in love with Vince. She was in love with her fantasy husband.

Jill overheard Spencer give instructions for the group to complete one more assignment and then break for lunch. She had no more time to daydream.

VINCE WAS DOWN to his last set of loafers. So why was he hiking up a mountain on a fool's errand in fine Italian leather?

Clearly, he was a fool. His actions so far this morning kept pointing toward that fact.

He should be gone by now. Instead, he'd trudged around Jill's property for an hour, until he'd had nothing left to do but throw his suitcase in the Porsche and leave. He'd even put the key in the ignition. But he couldn't start the car. So he'd shed his jacket and taken a hike.

He continued up the steep slope, ignoring the increasing pressure on his lungs. Not that he was out of shape. He had to be approaching three thousand feet above sea level. This was no stroll, but he continued to climb because there was nothing else he could do.

Well, that wasn't true. He could turn around, drive into Railroad Stop and send the details of the deal to his grandfather. He could gas up and point his Porsche back to Vegas. In nine or ten hours he could be home again. Or at least in the house that Jill's parents had given them as a wedding gift.

But Jill wouldn't be there. She'd be here battling it out with Arnie.

It shouldn't matter. It wasn't his problem. What should count was that Vince's grandfather would welcome him back, hopefully with open arms and Vince could return to the business of running his grandfather's casino, dining at fine restaurants every night and hanging out with Sam.

Well, maybe not hanging out with Sam. Since Sam had married Annie earlier in the year and adopted her daughter, Maddy, Sam had turned into a bit of a homebody. Although Vince had become fond of Sam's family, he'd never understood the appeal of staying home until he'd met Teddy.

Part of knowing who you are is knowing what you want. Edda Mae's words returned. Vince did know what he wanted. He wanted it all—the job, the girl, the family. But that wasn't in the cards for him. The fact remained, aside from his grandmother, Vince had let down everyone who'd ever cared for him. He'd never been good enough for his father to love. Sam pitied him. His grandfather didn't trust him. Teddy thought he was a jerk. And Jill was scared of him physically.

Be honest. Edda Mae was full of advice, but sometimes you had to lie to others to protect them.

The incline got steeper. The rocks became more like boulders, the trees farther apart. The sun broke through the clouds and beat down on Vince's shoulders. A bird sang happily in the distance. And the path dwindled to more of a goat trail. Vince knew about goat trails because he hadn't spent all his time in Iraq in Baghdad.

"This path leads to the top of the mountain," Vince quipped irritably, affecting Jill's casual tone. "I suppose she considers this a Sunday walk."

Vince was scrambling over rocks nearly the size of his car. He stopped to loosen his tie. He hated ties, but they were an occupational hazard of wearing dress shirts. Instead of yanking an inch or two out of the Windsor knot, Vince slid the tie off and stuffed it into his pocket. The cuffs of his shirt were filthy. At the top of the next boulder he removed his cuff links and rolled up his sleeves.

Vince reached the summit. From here he looked out over the valley to the south where Railroad Stop had been built, although he could only make out one rooftop. The rest were hidden behind a forest of pines. And if he faced west, he could see the undulating terrain stretching out to the central valley of California, shrouded in the distance by a thin layer of brown smog. The views were grand, making Vince feel insignificant.

Self-respect. Friendship. Love. Who was he to want so much out of life?

His BlackBerry started coming alive at his hip. Apparently he'd climbed high enough to get a signal.

There was a flapping of wings as a bald eagle flew twenty feet above Vince.

E-mails came in. He checked his inbox. His grandfather's response was short. "Contracts in process." No congratulations. No "job well done." Nothing Vince had done these past few months had won his grandfather's approval. Nothing ever would.

Vince sat down on a rock overlooking the broad vista, determined to stay until he had answers to his questions. He stared out over the landscape. He felt the bumps of scarred skin beneath his shirtsleeve. He waited. And, of course, no answers came, so he sat and waited some more.

And discovered he didn't like silence.

"Argh!" he shouted.

He had to face facts. His grandfather didn't love him. Jill didn't love him. Even Teddy didn't love him. And the deal that had been almost a sure thing was most likely going to be a bust. Railroad Stop was a dead end.

And then a doe poked her head above the undergrowth to his left. She leaped onto the plateau with Vince, walking across it as if she had no fear of him. Her eyes were huge and trusting, the arch to her neck strong and graceful. For several minutes Vince watched her roam the summit.

A noise froze the doe in place. Laughter. Her ears swiveled as she tried to home in on it.

"Hide," Vince urged. He didn't want to share the deer with anyone else, and he suspected Jill had sent her clients to hike the *path*. "Hide," he repeated when the deer still hadn't moved.

Someone laughed again. The doe bounded past

Vince down the west side of the mountaintop just as two of the credit-union managers reached the rise on the north side.

Vince tugged down his sleeves. "How did you get up here?" he asked. "I had to climb from the south."

"Jill told us to look for the trailhead at the split tree," the man explained, taking in Vince's ruined clothes.

"Ah, she must have forgotten to explain that to me." *Forgot, my eye.* Vince bid the newcomers farewell and headed back down the trail.

Edda Mae had been wrong. It didn't matter who you were. You had to know what you wanted, accept what you could get and then hedge all your bets.

Vince stopped and sent an e-mail to his lawyer about that divorce Jill wanted.

JILL CAUGHT SIGHT of Vince coming down the trail. He looked almost as bad as the day they'd posted the signs. His hair was mussed and his face sweat-streaked. His clothes were covered in filth and he may have wrecked another pair of shoes.

Vince slid into his car.

This is it. He's leaving.

She should turn away. But she couldn't. She needed one last look. As soon as Vince left, she would take off her ring and let go of silly fantasies and of her real husband. It was time to stand on her own.

Then Vince got out, opened the luggage compartment and took out his suitcase. He saw Jill watching him from the downstairs kitchen window and nodded once in acknowledgment before disappearing upstairs.

He must have found the answers he was looking for on his hike. Jill had answers of her own.

Vince was sexy and smart. He understood what it was like to hide your hurt and carry on. He did dishes and didn't leave the toilet seat up. Teddy adored him—well, most of the time anyway. And if Arnie was to be believed, Vince had passed up a very lucrative deal for Jill. If he wasn't the ideal husband, Jill didn't know who was.

Something pleasant spread through her chest, bringing a smile to her face and a renewed burst of energy. She was certain that everything—Shady Oak, Railroad Stop, her marriage—was going to be okay.

Why wouldn't it? Vince was going to be by her side.

VINCE ROLLED HIS EYES. Jill was crazy to have let Edda Mae leave her alone with all these people. She was damn lucky he hadn't gone today. Oh, he'd climbed into his car fully expecting to drive away, but then he'd realized Jill might need an extra hand. And, boy, had she ever. He'd grilled forty hamburgers and done the dishes, mountains of dishes. He'd read Teddy a bedtime story and tucked him into bed.

He was exhausted. Jill must be dead on her feet. She'd run around more than he had, with a smile on her face for every guest.

And oddly enough, a warm smile for him, too.

With his head propped on the unyielding arm of the couch, Vince sprawled half-on, half-off the short, narrow torture device in Jill's apartment waiting for her to lock up downstairs. He had to tell her about the deal he was setting up and that he was leaving in the morning. Before he went, he'd also tell her to expect divorce papers.

"Vince! You're still awake." Jill breezed in, glowing as if she'd just spent a day being pampered at the spa. She leaned over and pressed a kiss to Vince's forehead as she passed.

Vince grabbed the back of the couch to keep himself from falling to the floor.

"Thanks for helping me today," she said. "If not for you I'd still be elbow-deep in dirty dishes and never would have been able to read Teddy a bedtime story." In the kitchen Jill squirted lotion on her hands and massaged it into her skin with strokes that inspired Vince's overactive imagination. "I assume you're still up because you want to talk."

"Er…yeah."

"And Teddy's asleep?"

"Not a peep out of him." Vince smiled fondly. When Teddy had come home from school, all Vince's transgressions had been forgotten. Teddy was more excited to see him than he could ever have imagined.

"It's great to see you smile. I thought the walk up the hill might do you good." Jill sank into the chair next to him, bringing her smile and the smell of lemon lotion with her.

Frowning, Vince sat up. "Hill? It's a mountain. And given that you have to crawl the last fifty feet or so, I wouldn't go telling your guests it's a walk."

"Did I forget to mention you need to cut around to the left at the base of the summit?" Her blue eyes glinted with laughter as she kicked off her tennis shoes.

Once he confessed, how long would it be before she'd smile at him like that again?

"Right. At the split tree? You are evil, *wife*."

"Oh." She waved him off. "Edda Mae would have done the same thing if she wanted you to think."

And the bitch of it was, Vince believed her.

"Tell me about your scars." Jill's voice softened as she reached out to take his left hand.

Trapped. Vince didn't want to tell Jill anything. He didn't want her pity. But a trail of warm, fuzzy hope was humming its way up his arm from the hand she held.

"Share your secrets," Jill prompted.

And then Vince understood. Perhaps if he told her his secrets, she might trust him enough to make love. Would she? *Could* she even if she wanted to? And suppose if what he told her was a turnoff? His history was pathetic. "I'm not sure where to begin."

"You said on Friday that your dad was rough with you," Jill said gently.

"Rough?" Vince laughed, but it was an empty sound.

"Was it that bad?"

"No matter how hard I tried to please my dad, I was never good enough. He beat me from the time I was five. He beat me," Vince repeated, rubbing his forehead, hating that he sounded like a victim, but saying anything else was a lie. *A lie.* Edda Mae...

Vince strove to keep his voice light. "I learned the warning signs—slurred speech, loud voice, the swagger in his step. I developed the habit of blocking his blows with my left arm or turning my back so he'd hit me where no one else could see. That way I could still write, still go to school." Where he could see Jill, where he could pretend everything was okay.

"My dad was smart. I had to be smarter. And for a time, I was. But then I gained some height and he caught on to what I was doing. And that's when he started hitting me in the face."

"I thought you'd lost a lot of fights with other boys over girls you slept with," Jill said apologetically. "You had quite a reputation in middle school."

Vince glanced up at her. "Thanks for not telling me that sooner." Why would Jill have agreed to marry such a loser?

Then Jill made up for it by saying, "But I always told my friends I'd heard you put the other guy in the hospital."

"You always did have that loyal streak."

"I couldn't bear the idea of you losing," she admitted with complete seriousness.

"During those middle-school years I was harder for him to catch," Vince said. "But then I made a huge mistake. I placed a side bet on one of my grandfather's blackjack games and lost. When my dad found out about it, he went ballistic. My grandfather realized what happened and took me in. The next thing I knew, my parents had moved to Florida without me, didn't even say goodbye. I tried to run away, go after them, because I just knew if I tried to be perfect, my dad would love me."

"Don't," Jill said, tears in her eyes. "He should have loved you regardless."

"My grandfather came after me and for a while everything was okay. But I still dreamed about the day my dad would come back sober and be happy to see me. He'd apologize and we'd be a family again." What a waste of brain power that had been.

"Vince—"

"I had my happy ending. I finished high school, got married." Vince jiggled her hand in an effort to lift the mood. "And graduated from college. But I wasn't ready to…" He'd almost said *settle down.* "Whatever. I joined the army and was sent to Iraq."

"Your scar isn't that bad." Jill gazed at him as if she had X-ray vision and could see through his clothing.

"Looks are deceiving." His smile was weak, but it was better than breaking down and crying in front of her. "The first day out we were watching a parade. These men marched along with toddlers—*babies really*—strapped to their chests. This one little boy was sucking on his fist and grinning at me. I don't think I registered the man carrying him pulling out a gun and opening fire." His cheeks were starting to hurt with the effort of his smile.

"I choked. I couldn't shoot." Vince hadn't meant to tell Jill that. He'd never told anyone that. He hadn't even admitted his cowardice to Sam, and he'd *been* there. Was that another lie? Aw, hell, he owed Edda Mae an apology.

"I would have been a sitting duck, except my best friend, Sam, who'd been in the country a lot longer than I had, started firing his M16 and saved my life." Vince had to stop and swallow. It wasn't just terrorists who died that day. The children…

Jill's face seemed pale, as if she, too, knew that an M16 was not a precision instrument.

He continued lightly, as if relating a story about his time at college. "Anyway, while I did my impression of a statue, a sniper's bullet ripped through my arm. The force of it sent me to the ground. Other people weren't so lucky. The wound wasn't severe enough to send me home. They stitched me up, let me recuperate a bit and then sent me back out. If it wasn't for the scar, you'd never know what a coward I'd been."

Jill blinked, opened her mouth to speak, and then swallowed. When she did manage to string some words together, they came out barely above a whisper. "Would someone have called me if you...if you..."

"You're listed as my next of kin. If those Tangos had been better marksmen, you wouldn't need divorce papers." He tried to smile.

"Stop it. This isn't a joke." Her eyes shone with something awfully close to pity.

"The hell it isn't." Vince stood, severing the connection between them. Damn hope for making him think that the truth would break down the barriers between them. "It's a twist of fate, the irony of the universe. Someone somewhere is laughing at this, at my life."

Jill shook her head. "You didn't run away. You made it home alive."

"And I learned the hard way what I had to do to stay that way." Vince remembered the face of every man he'd ever killed. The ones he'd seen, anyway.

"What do you want, then? What does Vince Patrizio think fate, the universe or God owes him?"

"Nothing. All I wanted..." Vince swallowed thickly and tried again to be a man who wasn't weighed down with so much emotional baggage. "All I ever wanted...was for someone to accept me as I am. No conditions. No *If you do this, I'll love you.*" Vince had to confront his own truth, pathetic as it seemed.

"The deal you offered me in town was conditional," Jill said evenly, not quite rubbing it in his face.

"Yeah. I guess when so much crap happens to you, you have no choice but to adopt those same crappy ways." Vince was just like his grandfather, manipulating everything in his path. He supposed it could have been worse. Vince could have taken after his father— a drunken bully.

Jill stood. "Will you show me?" She took a step toward him.

"No." Vince turned away. Why wasn't she running? Vince hadn't been good enough to be loved as a kid or brave enough to take a life to save his friend. He was too pathetic for words.

Vince couldn't show Jill. She was right. It didn't look bad to others, only to him. He'd bared his soul, opened his old wounds. He needed to crawl into a hole and put his armor back on, not prolong this agony.

"I'm going tomorrow." Vince wanted to curse when his voice shook. "My business here is done." He turned away from Jill and went to the window.

It was the hardest thing he'd ever had to do—stand with his back to Jill as she left him.

CHAPTER FOURTEEN

VINCE WAS STILL AWAKE. Jill could hear him moving about the living room while she sat at her bedroom window looking out over the moonlit valley. It had been a successful day for Shady Oak. Edda Mae had called earlier to let her know she'd arrived safely in Fresno. She sounded happy. Jill should have been happy, too, and sound asleep.

Instead, she was bringing out the old memories of Vince and aligning them with the man in her living room. Then and now Vince always had an argument, a reason why she shouldn't do whatever it was she wanted to do. And he'd always kept his distance, choosing to come closer on his terms, when it was safe. Now Jill understood why. When he was a kid, he'd had enough physical hurt in his life without getting emotionally hurt by other children, who could be insensitive and cruel.

There was no point in Jill getting up. No reason for her to leave the bedroom. Vince wasn't going to open up to her. Tomorrow he'd be gone. And someday soon they'd get a divorce.

Jill padded down the hall in a pair of bunny-patterned pajama bottoms and her yellow tank top, paus-

ing at the edge of the living room. Vince was easily dis-
cernible standing next to the window in the moon-
light. He'd been looking down over the same view of
the valley. At least, she assumed that was what he was
doing, but then he shifted and rubbed his right biceps,
lifting his arm as if he could see through the material
of his T-shirt.

"It takes a strong man to bear scars like yours," Jill
said softly, stepping into the room, unable to let him
endure his pain alone.

Vince turned to watch her approach.

"Does it still hurt?" Jill nodded at his arm, knowing
it was a stupid question.

"Does it matter?"

"Yes."

Vince sighed. "I'm branded with a constant reminder of my failures, of my cowardice."

"I see it as a mark of perseverance, of forgiveness
and love." Jill was close enough now to touch Vince's
fingers with hers, twining them together when he
didn't protest. "Will you show me?"

"No." His refusal rasped across the air between
them, a warning to keep her distance.

But Jill was tired of friendship and empty beds.
She'd clung to the memory of one bad encounter for
too long. It was time to make a new memory. Now.
Tonight. Before Vince left in the morning.

"Please." Jill led Vince to the couch. When he
didn't protest she turned on the lamp on the end
table behind him, not surprised to find his eyes
searching her face. "May I?" Her hands hovered over
his right wrist.

Again Vince didn't protest. She pushed his sleeve up, but the knit cuff was tight and didn't slide over his forearm. With a sigh, Vince tugged his shirt off, his gaze returning to her.

Cords of taut muscle defined every inch of his arms and chest. But she sought out the round, reddish-brown scar in the front of his right arm, and the exit wound in back. Jill passed her palm over Vince's warm skin from shoulder to elbow, then she rubbed her forefinger and thumb over each scar.

Jill shifted her attention to his other arm. She could picture Vince as a young boy trying to stand up to his father with his left arm raised against another blow. There was a spot or two where the skin was discolored slightly, as if it had been bruised to the bone.

She pushed Vince back into the corner of the couch so that she could see his chest.

"Nothing on the front," he said gruffly.

Jill stood and went around behind him, needing to see his back. Vince had an oblong mark running several inches along his lower spine. "What's this?" she demanded.

"My dad threw me against a wall."

"And your legs?"

"My legs are fine."

She wanted to believe him. It was worse than anything she'd imagined. He'd not only faced death courageously in Iraq, he'd been abused as a child. Jill came back around the couch and sank to the floor at his feet, wrapping her arms around her knees. He'd been a little boy. What kind of man could hit a child, especially his own? "And your mother?"

"Too drunk. I think she was his target until I got old enough."

Extending one hand, Jill laced her fingers with his. "Why didn't you tell me?"

"Nobody wants pity, Jill. You, of all people, should know that." He kept his gaze averted.

"What I'm feeling isn't pity. It's anger—at your parents, at the warmongering ways of men, at you for not telling me sooner." Jill tried to contain this anger, tried not to let her next words quaver. "You would have had to tell me on our wedding night."

He cocked an eyebrow at her.

Jill swallowed her pride. He'd admitted he'd been with other women. Of course, he hadn't married her out of love and she'd been the one to leave. And he'd said he'd waited for her to contact him. Jill had to believe he hadn't lied about that. "Your girlfriends must have seen—"

"You'd be amazed what you can do with your shirt on." Self-loathing clouded his eyes as Vince pushed away from her.

Jill recaptured Vince's hand.

Vince stared at their joined hands and shook his head.

"They were fools," she repeated adamantly, knowing now that it had only ever been sex for Vince, nothing like the intimate ritual between a man and a woman in love.

"Go back to bed, Jill."

"No." She was trying to scrunch up the courage to gather him in her arms.

Vince's fingers closed painfully tight around hers. "You already heard my secrets. You know how I want

it to end. If you sit here and look at me like that, I'll…"
He paused to catch his breath. "I'll be asking a few
questions of my own. Like what really happened with
Craig." The bitterness she'd been expecting finally
surfaced in his words, echoed in his dark eyes. He
wanted to scare her away.

Vince loosened his grip, waiting for her to decide.

A week ago she would have run away from the
challenge. Jill rubbed the side of her face on her
shoulder, brushing away a tear. It would probably be
easier for both of them if she did as he asked. "I
suppose that's fair," she whispered, lifting her gaze to
his. "But my price is a kiss."

Vince wanted more than that, but he drew her
tenderly onto his lap and pressed his lips to hers once,
reverently. His chest was bare and she wore only that
skimpy tank top and pajama bottoms, so he had to
keep his distance, keep his head.

"Is that all?" Jill asked in a small voice, tucking her
head into the crook of his neck, sending her warm
breath across his skin.

"Kisses have to be earned," Vince said solemnly.
She fit nicely in his arms. He couldn't think about
other places he would fit for fear of losing control.
"What was the worst thing about the night with
Craig?"

"The shame." Jill sounded annoyed, her hand traveling slowly up his left arm. "The shame of doubting
my ability to love the baby. The shame of no longer
being perfect or invincible. He stole so much more
than my virginity."

"But he gave you a precious gift—Teddy." Vince

slid his hand up Jill's spine and back down again, mirroring her movement on his arm. If she noticed his erection pressing into her hip, she didn't mention it. "Did he ever try to contact you?"

"I sent him a letter after Teddy was born, notifying him that he was a father and asking him to sign away all parental rights. I heard back within a week." Jill snuggled closer and Vince held his breath. "That's enough talk about Craig. You certainly earned your keep today."

"You would have finished the dishes eventually, but I'm sure you would have multitasked and burned the burgers." Vince fought his body's impulse to tremble. Jill was in his lap. She hadn't locked herself in her room at his confession of weakness. Only, things probably weren't going any further than that chaste kiss. "I wish you'd said yes to a date with me that night, instead of meeting Craig." He'd known what Craig was like, how he targeted less-popular girls, the ones with such low self-esteem they wouldn't say anything later.

"I'm sorry." Her hand stilled. "I was blind."

And she'd paid the price. "I'd love to ask you out on a date now." One that ended up with them in bed.

Jill sat up and grinned at him. "Have you ever seen those old Dating Game shows? Bachelor Number Three—if we were stranded on a desert island, where would you take me for dinner and what would you wear?"

Now Vince could see where Teddy got his bad sense of humor. "It wouldn't be dinner. It would be an early breakfast watching the sunrise and the dolphins swimming in the surf. And clothing would be..." He couldn't bring himself to say optional, but she only smiled wider, so he didn't have to complete the sentence.

"You, my friend, have earned yourself another kiss." Jill shifted, causing another breath-holding moment. But she lifted her lips to his and claimed him as gently as if it was Vince who had been sexually abused, not her.

Her palms found their way to his chest, sliding down to his waistband in a tantalizing motion that had him pulling her toward him until he realized what he was doing. "I'm sorry." He started to release her, afraid he might scare her.

"Don't stop," Jill murmured against his mouth, wrapping her arms around his neck and drawing him closer until they were sliding down on the couch and Vince lay half on his side.

"Jill...I...are you sure this is a good idea?" he breathed against her ear. There was no place he'd rather be than cradled between her thighs. But knowing there'd be no follow-through, he thought they should slow down.

"You said I could have my wicked way with you." Vince could feel Jill grinning, her cheek plumping against his lips, and then she was shifting until her thinly covered body was pressed flush against his, their legs bent and cramped on the short couch.

"I don't think I said it quite like that." But damn if it didn't sound like his idea of heaven.

Jill froze, closed her eyes tight. Then she began disentangling herself from him. "Forget it."

"Whoa. Wait a minute. I'm not rejecting you. I could never reject you," Vince hurried to reassure Jill.

He needed her as badly as he needed air. "You own me, Jill. You have since our first day in kindergarten."

"Why does it sound like a *but* is coming?"

"*But* you kiss me like you want more and you have to tell me what kind of more. I mean, are we talking second base? Third?" *All the way?* He had a pounding erection that demanded to know Jill's intentions.

She sighed, her eyes still locked down. "I can't answer that. I just know that if I don't touch you tonight, if I don't learn the way you taste, the way you smell...I will have missed the greatest opportunity of my lifetime."

"Look at me, Jill." Vince pulled back as far as he could, given that the couch was made for someone Teddy's size.

Her eyelids didn't budge.

"Open your eyes, babe. Please. I want you to look at me." So he could gauge how serious she was about this.

Slowly, Jill met his gaze, her blue eyes filled with longing and only a hint of apprehension.

"Just so we're clear. This is not about casinos or Craig or my grandfather. This is about you and me, right?"

"Do you interrogate every girl you seduce?"

"I'm not seducing a girl," Vince said. "A woman has just invited me into her bed—her rules, her fantasies, anything goes. All I have to know is when and where."

"Now." Jill shifted and rolled onto the floor. Not that Vince thought she meant to, but he wasn't going to so much as crack a smile. She recovered quickly, getting to her feet and reaching for him. "My room."

Vince kissed the back of Jill's hand before letting her draw him to his feet, his heart singing a chorus of hallelujahs. "Just tell me what to do...or not to do."

"I think I need you to shut up," Jill said. "I don't like men—or electronic devices—that come with too much instruction." She was smiling because she loved their kibitzing, but if Vince kept distracting her, she'd over-think things and they wouldn't get further than the first pitch.

"This is not a silent movie." Vince waggled his finger at her. "I want to know what you like and what to give you more of."

"There you go, destroying the moment again." Jill stopped in the middle of the hallway and faced him, whispering because Teddy was just down the hall. "Maybe this isn't—"

Vince closed in and stole her breath, crowding her, moving quickly but not too fast. He backed her against a wall. His hands found her breasts, circled, squeezed and then looped around to cup her behind. Jill's knees wobbled. Vince was on full power, phero-mones set to thrill. He kissed a trail of fire from just below her ear to her breastbone and back up the other side.

Clinging to him, Jill lost several moments as she slipped into a place of pure pleasure, where her fantasy Vince and this real-life version combined. And then she felt as if she and this über Vince were melding together, their hearts pounding fiercely, only for each other. At some point he'd claimed her mouth and her hands, one of which he guided down below his belt, cupping her palm around his...around him.

"This is what you do to me," he said in a low, husky voice.

"I'm not afraid," Jill whispered defiantly, pressing

her hand more firmly against him. But she was. A little. She ducked away, distracted by a vision of Vince naked and her...well, she was naked, too. But how to get to that point?

"You're thinking too much." Vince took a tentative step forward.

Jill smiled, backing up a step, then another. "I'm thinking about you naked."

"Maybe you haven't noticed." Vince looked down at himself. "But I'm already halfway in the buff."

"I'm wondering if you have tan lines." She had her hand on the frame of the door to her bedroom now.

"Italians don't get tan lines. We also like to wear silk undergarments." He gave her a sly glance as he reached for her.

But Jill was a step ahead and now fully in her room, standing next to the bed, where she'd dreamed about Vince for far too many nights. "Are you wearing silk now?"

"Of course." Vince followed her, in her territory now. He closed the door behind him.

Jill lit a candle by the window. "You can turn off the light, too."

"We're losing the spontaneity," Vince warned gently, but did as she asked, sending much of the room into romantic shadow. "Come here and tell me just how you were imagining I got naked."

"I think...I think..." Jill swallowed her uncertainty from the other side of the bed. This was so much easier in her head. "I took your clothes off."

"Thank God," Vince said, holding out his arms. "Have at me."

Jill would have run to him, but something in his eyes demanded she go slow and make him want it. She giggled, then laughed. "I'm not much of a seductress."

"You're seducing the hell out of me. I can't wait for you to touch me."

"Your eyes say something different." She was at the corner of the bed now.

"I also can't wait for you to take off something of your own, say, your top?" he asked hopefully. "It would give me something to look at while you undressed me."

Jill shook her head. "Too distracting." She stopped when they were toe-to-toe, so close she could feel his warm breath on her face. "Now. Where to begin."

He glanced down. "Considering I've got no shirt and no socks on, I'd say you start with the button of these very tight pants."

"You have such strong arms." She ran her hands slowly over each one. There was power in his limbs that the damaged skin couldn't hide.

"The pants?" he reminded her.

"Beautiful, really." She ignored him, tracing a path up his left arm with her tongue. "This arm saved your life and kept you with me at school, where I needed you."

Vince held very still.

Taking her time, Jill licked her way across his chest, then kissed the bullet's entry and exit wounds on his right arm. "And this one saved your life, by taking the bullet that dragged you to safety so that you could come back to me. If I were you, I'd put these arms on display every day." Jill looked up into Vince's eyes, so dark and filled with unshed tears.

"Thank you," he whispered hoarsely.

Jill's throat felt too tight to speak, so she only nodded, finally having the courage to bring her hands down to his waistband. She'd been half in love with the idea of Vince before, and now she could imagine her love was reciprocated. Except a man like Vince would never settle for a relationship without sex. Jill didn't care what he said to the contrary. All she had to do was free a button, urge a zipper down. Surely he'd do the rest.

"Don't." Vince's hands covered hers. "This doesn't feel right."

"How do you know?" Jill buried the crown of her head in his chest. Her cheeks were burning.

"Because this should be about what *you* want, not what *I* want." Vince sighed and set her away from him. "Turn around."

Great. Vince didn't want her to watch him walk out of here.

"Turn around, Jill." Vince spun his finger in a circle and Jill did as he asked. "Now. I'm going to take my clothes off and get into bed. What you do after that is up to you. If you decide to go sleep on the couch and leave me here...my back will thank you."

Jill's cheeks rounded in a big, grateful grin. "How do you always know what..." Jill wasn't sure if she meant *what was best for her* or *what she was thinking.* He'd certainly done both.

"I may not deserve forever," he said, "but I've been thinking about you and me for a long, long time."

Jill heard Vince slip beneath the covers. She should have realized he'd have thought through what she needed if their relationship ever became physical. He was always so considerate of others.

And when Jill turned around, Vince was just as she'd imagined he'd be, lying in bed with his arms propped behind his head, hiding his scars, that dimpled grin flashing at her. She could have stared at him for hours and been happy, if she knew he wasn't wearing a thing beneath her quilt. And he was staring back at her.

"Your eyes are huge," he said. "You look like a doe trying to decide what to do."

"When have you ever seen a doe?" She took an involuntary step toward him.

"I saw one today." Vince's gaze shifted to the ceiling. "She was amazing. Do you know that when a doe looks at you it's almost as if you can see right into her soul? I wanted to protect her from…from…I don't know what. It's the same way I feel about you." His dark eyes swiveled back to Jill.

He watched the change in Jill with amazement. One moment she was uncertain, nearly slouching with hesitation, and the next she was a siren looking for satisfaction, her chest held high and proud before her. Bunny-rabbit pants. A soft faded-yellow tank top. To him it was the most enticing lingerie. He was tempted to wipe the back of his hand across his mouth in case he was drooling.

Not yet. Hold back. Keep quiet. Vince's fingers flexed in his hair, itching to touch her breasts, the flare of her hips, the curls between her legs.

"You're staring at my bunny pants." Jill began crawling over him like a cat, tucking the quilt tighter around his legs with each movement of her hands and knees.

"Not anymore." He had a bountiful view of her cleavage.

Without another word Jill stretched out on top of him, pressing her body against his. The joy of looking at her was replaced with the ecstasy of her caressing him, of her mouth joining with his, of her hands exploring the exposed skin of his chest and arms. Only it was humbling how Jill touched him with such tenderness. It made him feel whole and forgiven.

If she only knew...

But Jill did know. He'd told her, fully expecting to be scorned and rejected, which would have made his leaving tomorrow that much easier. Instead, he'd discovered a love as strong as his. For Jill was loving him, strengthening him, bringing him to a place of peace he'd rarely been in his life until he knew her.

Vince had fallen under her spell like a greedy child who was finally going to be given a longed-for toy, had engaged in this strange stop-and-go foreplay, willing himself to be happy with whatever crumb she gave him, telling himself that he was healing her. What a huge, fat whopper of a lie. Jill was healing him.

A more noble man might stop here, gather his clothes and tell Jill that whatever they were doing wasn't right. That she wasn't ready. Vince's fingers clung to the hair on the back of his head so that he wouldn't touch Jill even when her breasts brushed his chin as she stretched up to kiss his forearms. Again and again.

It was hell being good.

Jill tugged at his lip with her teeth, sending a jolt of desire to an already needy part of his body.

But what if she *was* ready?

She wasn't. Most women would have moved on by now, would have paid attention to his more vital parts. It wasn't that he was ungrateful, but the slow rhythm of her movements over his hips had his balls aching, and he could see the swell of her breasts above her tank top and feel the tight buds of her nipples on his chest. He wouldn't be able to walk in the morning, much less drive a stick shift.

Stop whining. You promised her anything.

And he'd deliver, even if it meant *not* delivering his goods, in return for this one night with Jill.

All of a sudden, Jill shucked her tank top and then lay that pair of beauties on him. "You don't mind, do you?"

Vince moaned like the sex-deprived horny devil he was as Jill kissed her way down the side of his neck. If he opened his mouth any wider to speak, he was going to beg.

One of Jill's hands slid behind his head, twining her fingers with his. She didn't realize the Herculean effort it took not to flip her over and show her how two people really made love. She didn't realize...

Vince froze as one of Jill's hands slid beneath the covers, past his hip, over the top of his thigh and right into position as if she and his cock had previously been on intimate terms.

"You're so soft," Jill murmured, once again finding interest in his mouth.

"I'm hard as a rock," Vince growled against her

lips, fighting off irritability, his building tension and the bliss that she was finally touching him.

"I meant your skin. Down there." She gave him a good feel followed by a roll of her hip.

"You have skin," he said rather inanely, way past the point of logical thought.

There was a long pause filled only with heavy breathing—thank heaven not just his—and the sound of bodies moving against sheets.

"Then why don't you touch me?" she asked in a small voice.

The hand she wasn't gripping found one of her breasts, testing its weight and size in his palm. And then his hand was stroking fire through Jill, making her move with restless energy on top of him, making her want more. More of his touch. More of him pleasing her.

How? That was the burning question. Her cheeks were still hot from the mortification of asking Vince to touch her. But he'd done as she asked. He'd done as she asked. He'd done...

Jill moaned as Vince rolled her nipple between his thumb and forefinger.

"Lovers tell each other what they like with more than words," he whispered, once more reading her thoughts. "Sighs...body language...changing position."

She'd like to think what happened next was her body taking over. She slid onto her side next to Vince and arched her back as if to say kiss me there, where you just touched me with your hand.

"Making love is about giving and taking," Vince continued, barely flashing her a smile before bending his head to her breast and showing her how good giving could be.

All Jill could think about was the taking part. It had been years before she'd worked up the courage to buy a vibrator. Months to feel comfortable enough to use it on herself while envisioning Vince's face—because he was the only man she felt safe with—and several more to get it right. Now all she wanted was to take what Vince offered, live and in person.

His hand had moseyed down to the waistband of her pants, his thumb teasing beneath the edge.

Jill tensed, suddenly flooded with memories of Craig, of rough hands and harsh words, his body pressing her into the couch, telling her it was too late to stop, too late to change her mind. She couldn't seem to breathe.

But Vince's hands danced higher, his lips moved from one breast to the other. Vince was gentle, his touch loving, respectful. Jill relaxed, drew in some much needed air. Craig, Jill realized, had no place in her bed when Vince lay beside her. She loved Vince. How could she not when Vince knew her better than she knew herself? This was her husband, and she'd be damned if she'd let Craig steal another night from her.

Jill squirmed, trying to free her hands, which were tangled with Vince's body, with sheets and blankets.

"Talk to me." Vince pulled back and gave her space, along with a look that was both sad and concerned.

"I can't get these pajamas off." Jill rolled onto her back, twisting and kicking until the bunny pants went sailing across the room. "Now I'm ready."

"I'm afraid to ask for what."

Jill slid beneath the covers, rolled her naked self completely against his warm, loving body and said, "For everything you promised me on my wedding night."

"One perfect night." Vince took a good look at Jill. "I don't want to scare you, but I'm not a missionary type of guy."

"Me, neither." Jill hoisted herself on top of him, suddenly in charge.

CHAPTER FIFTEEN

"ARNIE TOLD ME about your deal," Jill said, limbs tangled with Vince's as the gray light of dawn streamed into the windows of her bedroom.

After a night of stop-and-start lovemaking—pausing as soon as Jill began to feel uncomfortable and then resuming when she was once more in control of her emotions—they'd woken up hungry for each other about twenty minutes ago. With one hand still between her legs, Vince's craving for her was just as strong as ever.

"I meant to mention it," Vince lied, except it wasn't exactly a lie since he *had* meant to talk to her about it at some point. He'd just gotten sidetracked.

"You didn't have to do that for me, but thanks, anyway." Jill snuggled closer, unaware that her words caused a knot of apprehension in Vince's gut.

What had Arnie told Jill? It sounded like he'd implied Vince had passed on the project.

"That's what love is about, isn't it? Sacrifice. Compromise." Her breath wafted over Vince's bare skin, but it was her words that gave him goose bumps.

"You love me?" Vince should have been drawing Jill to him, but that bit about Arnie still nagged.

Jill sighed. "Some people need the words." Then she pinched his rib cage. "I know you love me."

"Great, sure," Vince blurted. "Now let's get back to Arnie."

She looked at Vince as if he'd sprouted an abundance of nose hair. "Yes, but you couldn't have known I loved you. I didn't know it myself until yesterday."

Yesterday. Lies. Let it not be true. "About Arnie—"

"No." Jill sat up, taking the sheet with her to cover her breasts. "I refuse to bring Arnie into this. There are things that a woman holds sacred—her wedding day, the birth of her children and the moment she exchanges *I love yous*…though not necessarily in that order."

Vince gazed up at Jill, drank in her mussed-up hair and the spark in her blue eyes. He knew this would come. The end. Because Arnie…Arnie had said something to Jill and based on that, she'd decided she was in love with Vince.

Just one night. He'd always known it would be just one night.

"For once," Jill said. "For once I want that special moment without a caveat. Is it too much to ask?"

Vince shook his head. He couldn't give her that. Not today. Not ever.

"Say something. Why don't you say something?" No longer whispering, Jill was cranking up the volume.

"I made Arnie an offer yesterday morning," Vince admitted. "But I don't think that's what Arnie told you, is it?"

Blinking rapidly, Jill shook her head.

"What did Arnie say, Jill?"

She hung her head, auburn tresses hiding her face.

"Something about how he thought our businesses *could* have complemented each other."

Vince was going to kill Arnie.

"I thought you gave everything up for me," Jill said in a small voice.

The morning was chilly. Vince hadn't realized it before. Now everything was sharp and clear. Vince knew why Jill had come to him last night. She'd assumed he'd passed on the casino and done so because he loved her. And that had made her think she was in love with him.

"Is that why you were planning on leaving?" she asked, lifting those sky-blue eyes to his. "Because you had a deal with Arnie?"

"Yes." Vince should have gone yesterday. Then he wouldn't have had to watch Jill's heart breaking.

"You're still planning on leaving." Not a question.

"Yes." Vince reached for Jill's hand, unable to curb the compulsion to help her when he was dying inside. He was used to rejection. He'd survive. "You don't love me. Not really."

She shook off his hand. "You don't know what you're talking about."

"I do," Vince said sadly. "You need my wedding ring, not me."

"I just told you I loved you."

"Only because of something Arnie said. You thought I gave up everything for you and I didn't." Vince swallowed. He'd live at least another ten years replaying this morning in his head, knowing he did the right thing and hating himself for it.

"Last night—"

"Was a milestone in your recovery." Vince rolled out of bed, found his boxers and pants and pulled them on. He couldn't look at Jill and pretend he wanted this to be over. Vince needed his shirt, but he'd left it in the living room. He felt so exposed. "I can't see you moving back to Vegas. Can you imagine me staying up here?"

She chose not to fill the painful silence for what seemed like hours, while Vince gathered his memories of the night, of Jill, of what made her smile and what made her sigh.

Jill finally decided to play along. Her voice shook, but there was a note of strength there that had been missing before. "You'd never fit in here. Not with those suits of yours. You're right. It's best if you do leave now. After all, I don't want to be one of those pathetic women who expects more than one night."

"Jill, don't." Vince turned around. He had to see her face one last time.

"Don't? Don't what?" Jill had risen to her knees, the sheet still clutched under her armpits, a contemptuous curl to her mouth. "Don't make this awkward scene any more painful for you? I hadn't realized I was your special little sidebar project while you were in town. What were you going to do this morning? Drive off without telling me the truth?"

Vince knew it was time to go. But his feet weren't as convinced, maybe because his brain was clamoring to be heard, demanding he drop to his knees and beg for her forgiveness. But who was he kidding? He didn't have the guts. He'd failed at everything. Jill didn't love him. His grandfather didn't respect him. The casino deal would fall through.

"Get out." Jill sank down and turned away.

This time, Vince did as she asked.

JILL NEVER KNEW how she made it through the hours after Vince left. She had breakfast for twenty to make and a little boy to see off to school on the bus. She smiled. She chattered away with her guests, telling them where the best shopping was on the trip back down the mountain. No one guessed her heart was breaking.

Even after the last credit-union guest left, Jill kept going. There were beds to strip and remake, rooms to clean, loads of laundry to be done. If she stopped, Jill suspected she'd never be able to finish things up in time for the nuns arriving the next morning.

Teddy came home from school and called Edda Mae. Jill paced the apartment while he gave her all the news, dreading that she had to tell him Vince was gone.

"Moonbeam got out and chased the postman to the front gate before he realized it was only a little dog and chased her right back up to the porch. At first, Edda Mae was going to spank the postman, but she just scolded Moonbeam."

Throat shut nearly as tight as a clam, Jill managed to force out a high-pitched chuckle.

"When is Vince coming back, Mom?"

"He's..." Jill took a deep breath. "He's not coming back."

Eyes scrunched, Teddy didn't say anything for a second or two. "Ever?"

"I...no." Jill sank onto the couch and stared out the window, brought down by a feeling of loss so deep it was as if someone dear to her had died.

Maybe someone had. Maybe it was her fantasy Vince that had been eradicated this morning.

"Did you know girls can get chicken pox in their eyes?" Teddy asked in a small voice. He'd been so sure that Vince would be his dad. "Edda Mae says that's where Maria's got them. That's so wicked. I hope she keeps them until Halloween."

Jill had to bite her lip to keep from crying. She could always count on Teddy to try to keep her spirits up.

It wasn't until later that night when she was showering that Jill broke down and sobbed. She lay in a crumpled heap at the bottom of the shower until the water ran cold, trying not to believe that Vince was Craig, only with a smoother approach and longer timeline.

"VINCE? SAM, IT'S VINCE." With a huge grin, Annie Knight leaned her very pregnant body forward to give Vince a hug. "Did you just get back? Did you make your deal? Can you stay for dinner?"

"Annie, let the man in before we air-condition the whole neighborhood." Sam appeared behind his wife and waited for the front door to close before he gave Vince a back-slapping man hug.

The couple led him into a comfortably casual living room with an overstuffed couch—respectably long and deep—and leather recliner facing a big-screen television. Maddy, their six-year-old daughter, was playing blackjack with herself on the coffee table.

"Uncle Vince!" When she saw him, the future blond knockout raced over to hug Vince's leg.

Vince hadn't spent a lot of time with Sam and his family in the past year, but they'd vacationed together at Lake Tahoe the previous June, and Sam's ladies had won Vince over permanently.

"Do you like my new dress?" Maddy tugged at the hem. "It's got the queen of hearts everywhere. Did you know the queen is a ten in blackjack but a twelve in solitaire?"

"What about the king of spades, midget?"

"Ten and thirteen." Maddy spun around so her skirt flared out, then leaned in to his leg again and sighed. "Cards are so much fun."

Given the fact that her mother and grandfather had both been professional gamblers, Maddy's fascination with games of chance was no surprise. Her innocent enthusiasm reminded Vince of Teddy, making his smile that much harder to hold on to. "What about counting? I thought you loved counting."

"I love counting cards!" She laughed and skipped back to the coffee table.

Annie was reclining on the couch, positioning pillows on either side of her humongous belly. "Sorry. The doctor says I need to be horizontal as much as possible so the twins don't arrive too early."

"They look like they're going to be here tomorrow," Vince said, eyeing her with trepidation.

"Is your smooth compliment payback for me beating you at blackjack this summer?" Annie said, tossing her chin in the air.

"As I recall, I beat you the second round," Vince pointed out.

"Oh, we both know I threw that game because I love you so much."

"Pity for my card-playing skills is more like it."

"Did I hear the doorbell?" Ernie, one of Annie's honorary uncles, appeared in the hallway wearing madras shorts and a Grateful Dead T-shirt. He rubbed a hand over his stubby gray hair. "Vince, you're back."

"Good to see you, too." Vince gave Sam an inquisitive look.

"It was our turn to take him in." Sam sounded pained. The washed-up gambler never seemed to make enough money to stay afloat for long.

"I've got a legitimate job," Ernie countered.

Sam and Annie exchanged meaningful glances that Vince couldn't interpret. Reminded of his brief closeness with Jill, Vince looked away. Why had he felt compelled to stop here?

"Can I get you something to drink? Beer? Coffee?" Sam stood and headed toward the kitchen before Vince could find an excuse to leave.

"Coffee would be fantastic." Vince trailed after him.

"You look like hell," Sam said, taking in Vince's rumpled clothing once they were in the kitchen.

"I just drove back from Northern California." More than nine hours of driving had cramped Vince's muscles again, but that pain was nothing compared to what Jill must be feeling. Vince couldn't stop wondering how she was. "Drove straight through."

"Did you find what you were looking for?"

"Yes." He'd found his wife and made her love him, if only for one night. But it was over. Vince couldn't lie to himself anymore. Jill deserved someone whole and true. He couldn't even honor his wedding vows.

"Where is it?" Sam asked, filling the coffee grinder with fresh beans.

"What?"

Sam spoke slowly, as if Vince were an idiot. "Where is your casino going to be built? We are talking about your new project, aren't we?"

"Yeah."

"You are so full of it."

"I did make an offer. It's in Railroad Stop, California."

Sam frowned. "Why does that sound familiar? Where is that?"

"Gold country. Very remote. Beautiful really." Vince smiled ruefully. "I hope if the deal goes through, the developers don't take away its small-town charm."

Sam stared at Vince without speaking.

"What?"

Sam shook his head and turned on the coffee grinder. The smell of coffee wafted through the air, bringing back memories of Edda Mae's hot brew, of Edda Mae's stories and her squinty-eyed stare.

"What?" Vince repeated.

Sam poured the grounds into the coffeemaker. "You've just never really cared about any place before. It makes you sound grown-up." Sam stared at Vince again while the coffee began dripping into the pot.

"What now?" Vince demanded.

"I keep expecting you to call me a choice word."

"Like overinquisitive? Nosy?"

"Something more R-rated. Jeez, what happened to you?"

Wonderful. Now even his best friend didn't like him.

"He fell in love," Annie called from the next room. "Can't you tell? He looks like he's got the stomach flu."

Sam chuckled as he got down two man-size mugs. "Ignore her." Then he looked at Vince and did a double take. "She's right."

"It's not like that. I don't do love." Vince glanced at his left hand. What was he going to do with his wedding ring?

Sam snapped his fingers. "It's *her.* Your wife. That's why Railroad Stop sounded familiar."

"I showed you Jill's photo one time when we were in Iraq. How would you remember something like that?"

"I'm a private eye. I have a killer memory," Sam said with a sly smile. "Shall we break out a bottle of champagne?"

"He's not happily in love, sweetheart," Annie called.

"She's on the couch and she can pick up a signal out here," Sam muttered.

"Offer him whiskey," Annie said.

Vince shook his head. "Coffee will do. I'm not in love. In fact, I'm thinking about moving."

"I'm sorry, man. If you want to come over later and watch football or something, let me know. You logged in enough hours with me when—" Sam raised his voice so his wife was sure to hear him "—Annie got all crazy and tried to leave me."

"True love is like friendship, sweetheart. Sometimes you just need a little space."

"I never get the last word," Sam grumbled.

But Vince, who wasn't immune to the charm of their banter, had suddenly realized why he'd come by Sam's. "I need to thank you."

"For what?"

"For not calling me a coward in Iraq. For putting up with my bullshit when I thought my grandfather was Mafia. For being my friend and including me in your family." Vince paused and rubbed his right arm. "I haven't had a lot of friends. And family, well, that's pretty much hit or miss."

"Have you been drinking?" Sam asked, peering at him closely. "I mean, I respect what you're saying. You know I feel like we're brothers and, as for Iraq, to have something like that happen to you on your first day...it's not something they train you for. You reacted like a human being." Sam swallowed, his gaze ricocheting off everything but Vince, no doubt remembering he'd been the one to pull the trigger when Vince couldn't. "Quit beating yourself up over it. I'm not saying it doesn't still suck to remember that day, but neither one of us deserves to let it ruin our lives."

Vince managed a miniscule nod and breathed a little easier.

"You know," Sam said, back to examining Vince's face. "You're not usually so..."

"Honest?"

"Yeah." Then Sam smiled. "But, hey, women do that to you. They push and they push until your demons don't seem so bad."

Which would be just fine with Vince, but he was afraid that Jill hadn't appreciated such honesty this morning, and wouldn't until she met the man who'd make her happy for the rest of her life. Which would be fine if Vince had been completely straight with her, but he hadn't. He'd hedged his bets before they made love.

And now he couldn't help but hope that Jill would overlook his lack of honesty.

Just this once.

JILL STOOD at the podium at the front of the room in the community center the Monday night after Vince left. There were thirty minutes before the city council meeting was to start. She had nothing prepared. No speech. No fact sheet. Nothing. She could only hope that the citizens of Railroad Stop who showed up tonight had strong opinions and ideas. Jill was fresh out.

She bent her head. She was so tired. The nuns had done it. Five days of silence and sign language and notes, four of which were without Edda Mae. Oh, Edda Mae had tried to talk to her about Vince, but mostly Jill kept it all inside. And it was eating her alive.

Had Vince really taken advantage of her? Or had Jill misread Vince's signals and been unable to reassure him that what they had was true love? She'd been fooled into thinking Craig liked her. Had she been fooled into thinking she loved Vince? It hurt too much not to be the real thing.

Vince said he'd been hers since kindergarten. But if that was true, wouldn't she have known it? Wouldn't he have expressed it in some way?

His father started beating him before Vince entered kindergarten. He probably learned to hide his feelings at an early age.

And she'd slept with Vince, her body tightening at the memory. He'd known exactly what to say to her about Craig. He'd known exactly how to treat her in the bedroom. He'd said he'd thought about it for a long time. But Vince was an experienced lover, had managed a load of practice while they were married.

But he said he was waiting for you to return to him. He promised to give you back what Craig had stolen. He said he thought other women would be repulsed by his scars and that the next person he showed them to would be his wife.

And then there was Teddy. Vince claimed he wanted to be his father, but left without saying goodbye and had sent no word in five days. Five days to a ten-year-old was a lifetime.

But Vince seemed to know what Teddy needed. His advice was spot on.

He was more successful than he allowed. He'd worked hard to put together a deal that would benefit his family's company. He survived Iraq. But he was certain everything he touched was destined to fail, and he'd used every setback as proof of how incompetent he was. Yet, Vince was a great negotiator, able to find common ground where there was none. With her. With Teddy. With Arnie.

Maybe Vince made the offer because he believed it wouldn't fly. Just by the fact that he was involved with it.

That couldn't be.

But...

It was just like Vince to sacrifice his own interests for Jill. He always put himself last, as if he didn't believe he was worthy of anything better. Which would mean that there was a strong likelihood he'd also tried to persuade Jill she wasn't in love with him. A few more days and Jill might not have been so vulnerable, but what she felt for him was still too new, too fragile to withstand Vince's attack. If he thought their marriage was doomed to fail again, he might not have wanted to take a chance on more than one night. Hadn't he said something about one perfect night?

No wonder she felt so betrayed. She did love Vince. And he loved her.

Wait until she got him alone in a room. She was going to tell him exactly how stupid he'd been, how brilliant, how annoying.

The door creaked open at the back of the hall. Jill whipped her head up, looked at the clock. Six-forty. It was about time people showed up for the meeting.

Edda Mae came in, Teddy on her heels. The door swung shut.

"I'm so sorry we're late," Edda Mae said.

Teddy dragged his feet up the aisle, touching a chair on each row along the way.

"It's okay, Edda Mae," Jill said, still staring at the clock. She'd gotten Vince into this mess all those years ago. She was the one person who loved Vince enough to make their marriage right. "Do you have Arnie's telephone number?"

Edda Mae squinted at her. Teddy froze in place.

"I'm the mayor and I ought to know what's best for this town." Jill gathered up her purse. "And what it needs is economic growth. If the casino is the best way to do that, then so be it."

"I thought we were against casinos," Teddy said.

Edda Mae nodded, for once at a loss for words.

"Not anymore. Come on. It shouldn't be hard to find Arnie. He's probably parking that enormous truck of his." Jill started toward them. Something in Edda Mae's hand caught Jill's eye. "What's that?"

Edda Mae looked stricken. "It's a…it's a…"

"FedEx package. From Vince. See?" Teddy pulled it down to his level. "It came after you left."

Jill understood Edda Mae's horror. She wanted to be sick. The only thing Vince could be sending in an envelope that size was divorce papers.

CHAPTER SIXTEEN

"IT'S ABOUT TIME you came to see me," Aldo said as he stood up to greet his grandson. He took a few faltering steps toward Vince, then hesitated.

"I had to take care of some things." After losing Jill, Vince had needed a few days to decompress and bolster himself for this most important meeting with his grandfather. Today he'd felt ready to face Aldo and see if the deal he'd struck with Arnie had met with the old man's approval.

Wearing khaki slacks and a long-sleeved button-down shirt, Vince stood in his grandfather's foyer, drinking in the familiar sights—the Picasso on the wall, the poker table, the grand view of The Strip. Vince had lived here when he was in high school. The only thing that seemed different was his grandfather. When Vince had left Las Vegas last year, his grandfather had been less robust but just as feisty. Now he seemed tired and frail.

Neither of them spoke for the longest time. Vince was used to a grandfather always in motion, shouting for quicker responses, better returns. This man was nothing like him.

Vince was suddenly afraid that his grandmother had passed away and no one had told him. "How is *Nonna?*"

"The same. We've had no incidents since the summer." The old man reached over and knocked his bony knuckles on the poker table. Periodically, Rosalie Patrizio's organs stopped functioning. It was only a matter of time before the doctors could no longer save her.

Again the awkward silence. Why wasn't Aldo asking him about the deal? "Can I see her?"

"Certainly." His grandfather deflated into his chair, not looking Vince in the eye.

On impulse, Vince went to stand in front of his grandfather, offering him a hand. "Come on. You, too. You know she always loved you best." It was an old joke of theirs.

Behind the thick trifocals, dark eyes sparked to life. "No-no. She loved you best, but she loved me the longest." He accepted Vince's help up and leaned on him as they walked toward the bedroom.

"How've you been, old man?" There had been times when Vince, in his frustration and self-centeredness, had used the term derisively. Not now.

"No one asks me how I've been."

Vince was suddenly struck by the silence, the loneliness of the penthouse. "I'm asking."

"I'm not through with this world yet, if that's what you mean." Some of the fire returned to his voice. "Always the smart one."

"Let's not fight." Vince pushed open the door to his grandparents' bedroom suite. Over by the window a hospital bed surrounded by softly whirring machines contained the thin shell of his grandmother. "She wouldn't approve."

The private nurse on duty stood and quietly left the room.

It seemed to Vince that they took a long time crossing from the door to the bed and it wasn't just because his grandfather walked slowly. Vince's feet dragged, as well.

"You look beautiful today, Rosalie." His grandfather reached over and stroked her short, silver hair, then he perched on the edge of the mattress.

Vince took his grandmother's hand. "It's me, Vince." He frowned. "She looks so tired."

His grandfather nodded, his lips pursed, his hands clasped in his lap, yet shaking. How could Vince ever have doubted the love his grandfather had for his grandmother? Aldo Patrizio would do anything for his Rosalie. Vince wished *he* was capable of such love.

Vince knew he cared for Jill. She'd always hold a special place in his heart. He wanted the best for her and that was why he'd given her up. Vince could imagine sitting on the edge of Jill's bed fifty years from now, talking to her as if she was still cognizant of his presence, making sure she knew he was still in love with her as she slipped away.

Vince stopped breathing. He was in love with Jill?

Oh, hell. He was. He had to be. Vince stared at the ceiling and shook his head. He'd screwed things up again.

Unless Jill loved him with the depth of emotion his grandfather felt for his grandmother. There was only one way to find out. And that was to wait and see how she reacted to the divorce papers.

Vince turned his attention back to his grandmother. "I have to tell you a couple of secrets, *Nonna*. One you probably already know and the other I'm sure you don't. But I'm not going to lie to you anymore." And then Vince started to roll up his sleeves as he told his grandparents how his arms had come to be less than perfect and how his heart had finally healed.

"Is that a new desk?" Vince asked later, after he and his grandfather had wiped away their tears and hugged each other.

"It is. The gadgets on top are new, too." His grandfather hesitated. "I don't know how to work any of them. Some new *jamook* in the computer department downstairs thought I needed it all. And then the management team agreed with them."

Vince grinned. Kudos to the old man for trying. "You don't have to use the latest technology to prove you're a smart man, *Nonno*." It had been years since Vince had used the Italian endearment for his grandfather.

His smile was pleased. "I've got a new executive assistant. Ernie. You might remember him. He was one of those cardsharps we were looking for last year. He works everything electronic for me, types it all, too—correspondence, e-mail. I swear he doesn't listen to a thing I say. You know me. I say what I say and I say what I mean some more and then Ernie only writes one sentence. Everyone's happy to hear less from me, I suppose."

"Ernie's been typing your e-mails?" Vince smiled. That explained the terse messages he'd been receiving.

"Yes, the *jamook*. He reads the incoming ones, too, prints them and organizes them into color-coded files. What man my age has color-coded files?"

"Did you know I made an offer to the Amador tribe over a week ago?"

"Of course, I know. It was a magnificent first-round deal. They haven't countered yet, but we won't budge."

"I don't expect them to counter." The fact that Vince had made an offer he knew would stalemate the casino troubled him. Railroad Stop needed something, but he'd decided Jill's plan would more directly benefit the population. "I'm not going to look for any more deals. You don't need another project. I know that breaks our contract, so I'll find a job here in town where I can be close to you."

"I don't want you to work anywhere else." His grandfather tilted his head up to look Vince in the eye. "I'm very proud of you. Even if you'd never found a deal, I'd have been proud of you and would have loved you just the same."

Even though he'd waited a lifetime to hear a member of his family say that, Vince couldn't resist contradicting his grandfather. "I've been an ass, especially to you."

"I wish you would use your Italian to curse. It shows so much more class." Aldo chuckled. "*Strunz*. You were a *strunz*."

Calling Vince a piece of shit was the perfect olive branch. He was, after all, very much like his grandfather.

"I'M TOO LATE." Jill pulled into the driveway of the house she and Vince owned in Las Vegas. A truck filled with two wardrobe boxes was parked in the middle of the driveway and left barely any room for her car.

It was five o'clock on a sweltering Sunday and her little sedan's air-conditioning had given out about an hour before. Her dress stuck to her back and legs.

But Jill hadn't come this far for nothing. She knew Vince loved her. She tried to slip on her sandals, but her feet were swollen from the combination of the ninety-degree heat and the soda she'd bought when she'd had to roll the windows down fifty miles ago.

Jill got out of the car barefoot, toting her purse and a stack of papers as she ran for the lawn. She'd forgotten how hot Las Vegas pavement could be in September. She cooled her tootsies in the blades of grass and pried the damp blue cotton from her backside as she surveyed her wedding gift.

The house looked the same—much too grand with its columns in front, red-tile roof and large windows. The shrubs lining the walkway were neatly trimmed and the yard well maintained. Vince had taken good care of their house. So why was he moving?

"You have too many clothes." A man's voice. Unfamiliar. Coming from the garage.

"I don't," Vince countered. Jill's heart began to pound. "Just because you live in shorts and polo shirts doesn't mean everyone else does."

"You have more clothes than Annie does." The speaker was walking backward carrying one end of a wardrobe box. He was taller than Vince. Lankier, too.

Jill decided the best way to get Vince's attention was to jump in. "I know he has more clothes than I do."

The back end of the box dropped.

"Hey." The man in front fought against being crushed.

"Jill?" Vince appeared wearing Bermudas and a T-shirt. Short-sleeved, no less. He looked fantastic and it was all Jill could do not to fling herself into his bare arms, especially when he gave her a hesitant smile and a slow once-over. "What are you doing here?"

Jill smiled and waved the divorce papers. "Apparently they need to be notarized in Nevada." It might have been a lie. Jill hadn't done more than stare at the top page. She had no idea what she was supposed to do with them if she really wanted to divorce Vince.

"Oh?" His gaze turned wary.

"You going somewhere?" Jill asked, pointedly glancing at the boxes already packed. She hadn't counted on that. Was there something in the divorce papers about the house? She should have read them.

"Yeah. I'm moving out."

Jill forced herself to keep smiling.

"I'll go back inside where it's air-conditioned," tall and lanky said. "I'm Sam, by the way. I take it you're Jill."

"Nice to meet you." Jill gave a little wave and then waited until Sam left them alone.

A classic red Corvette rumbled past, then backfired. Vince barely flinched.

"You look great," Vince said, coming a few steps closer and wiping his brow.

"It's a new dress. Do you like it?" Jill would have spun around if she wasn't convinced the cotton on her back was a different color from being drenched with sweat.

He'd taken another few steps, his gaze in the area of her cleavage. For the first time in years Jill was showing some skin. No flannel shirts or loose-fitting tops. She felt pretty.

"I do. Like it, that is." Now that she was closer she could tell his arms had the beginnings of a tan.

"So, you're moving…um…where?" She wanted to ask *why* he was moving. This ruined everything.

"Back to my grandfather's penthouse at the Sicilian. He has trouble getting around and I thought…" He sighed. "It's really great to see you. How's Teddy?"

"Good. He's going to paint the scenery for the school play. He's very excited."

"Really? And Edda Mae?"

"She's good, too."

"And Looney?"

"You don't really want to know about Moonbeam, do you?"

He shook his head, then grinned at her. "You don't have to get those divorce papers notarized in Nevada."

"I don't?" Jill glanced at them as if just a quick look would enable her to figure out all that legalese.

"No. Have I told you how great you look in that dress?"

"Not nearly enough times." The sun felt so hot it stole Jill's breath.

Vince stopped about five feet away from her. Five feet too far. "Why are you really here?"

Jill sighed. He always saw right through her. "It all started with Arnie."

"Arnie?"

"Uh-huh. He didn't think your deal was very fair. In fact, he recommended that the tribe turn it down."

"Oh." Vince looked superior. Jill had known it was exactly what he wanted all along.

"And then I told him the tribe couldn't turn it down."

"You what?" Vince walked in a tight circle, then

jabbed his finger at her. "Now look, Jill, you're muck-
ing things up."

"I went over the details with Arnie and I thought he
could do better."

"Why would you do that?"

Jill sighed again, but this time slowly, followed by
a carefully rehearsed explanation. "Because I'm the
mayor and Railroad Stop needs a casino, as well as
vacation homes, to bring the town back to life. In fact,
I'm considering changing the name to Railroad Go.
That's how positive I am that we're going to turn the
place around." She smiled brightly.

A muscle jumped in Vince's jaw. "I went to a lot of
trouble to make sure that deal didn't go through." He
had to be the trickiest, most intelligent man Jill knew.

"I know. That's why I had to step in."

Vince washed a hand over his face and looked around
the yard as if it could provide him with answers. Finally
he brought his gaze back to Jill's. "I'm confused."

"I'm so glad." It was payback time. Jill put her
hands on her hips and raised her voice. "Because I was
more than confused when you gave that Oscar-winning
performance the morning you left me. I have never met
a man more certain that he's worthless than you are and
I've never known a man more noble and brilliant and
courageous."

Vince was shaking his head.

"Oh, get off your high pity-me pony," Jill snapped,
really warming up now. "Failure? You? You out-
smarted a Stanford graduate millionaire and probably your grandfather, as well. You saved Teddy's life
when you caught him on those rapids. You deserve

everything your heart wants, including to be loved unconditionally." Jill prayed his heart wanted her.

Vince was close enough to touch now, grinning with that dimple that she loved so much, but Jill was still too wound up to stop.

"Who gave you the right to decide that you can just waltz in and out of my life whenever you please? I told you I loved you." Her voice dropped. "I showed you."

"You certainly did." Vince put his hands on her shoulders and warmth seeped immediately to her core.

"I think I was half in love with you when we got married." And she'd nurtured the feeling for years. "And then you broke my heart."

Vince slid his hands around to her backside, cocking one eyebrow. "You're wet."

"My air conditioner broke. I need to shower and change."

His grin was positively wicked as he lowered his head toward hers.

"That's it. I'm leaving," Sam said, coming out of the garage. "Why should I pretend not to watch you make out when I can go home and make out with my wife? Call me when you're serious about moving."

Jill stumbled back, having forgotten that Vince was leaving their house to help his grandparents.

Vince frowned, not taking his eyes off Jill, but now his eyes were filled with regret. "I *am* serious. My grandfather needs someone there with him. Someone who can go to the meetings or just keep him company."

"Is there room in the penthouse for two more?" Jill asked optimistically.

"No," Vince said. "There are two extra bedrooms, but the nursing staff shares one of them."

"If you're not dead set on living with your grandfather," Sam said. "I know someone who's looking for a place to stay."

Vince met Sam's speculative gaze. "Ernie? You can't be serious."

"It's your call." Sam threw up his hands. "It's either that or Ernie comes to live with Jill."

"If you need to stay with your grandfather, Vince, I'll understand," Jill said, more than a little depressed. "Teddy and I can live here. We could put Ernie, whoever he is, in the garage apartment."

"Wait a minute. You can't come to Vegas," Vince protested. "You run a successful business in Railroad Stop."

"I just *sold* a business. To Arnie. And Francie is moving back to help run it with Edda Mae. That way Francie can spend more time with her kids."

Vince held up his hands in surrender. "But that place was everything to you."

Jill shook her head. "It meant nothing without you. Teddy and I both agreed." Since Vince still looked shocked, Jill added, "And then Edda Mae had a story that fit the situation perfectly."

"Of course she did. But you're the mayor."

"Only until elections in November. I talked with Joe Mattwell, the baker? He's interested in running."

"So are you going to phone Ernie or not?" Sam demanded, flipping his car keys impatiently.

"I'll call him after you and I unload the truck," Vince said. "During which time Jill is going to go take a nice long shower."

WHEN VINCE JOINED Jill in the shower, he couldn't help thinking that it was amazing to be a couple, wonderful to be married, awesome to be a dad.

"Have I told you how great you looked in that dress?" Vince said as he climbed in.

"You didn't like my Shady Oak wardrobe?" Jill was trying to sound offended, but Vince wasn't buying it.

"It was hard to imagine your curves through all that flannel." Vince squirted some soap into the puff and began scrubbing Jill's back. Then he turned her around and washed her front.

Jill curled her arms around his neck, pouting to be kissed.

"Hey, I can't see what I'm doing."

She inched closer until her soapy breasts were pressed against his chest. Her amazing blue eyes half closed and got that distant look, the one that told Vince she liked the way things were going.

"You're right. I don't need to see what I'm doing," Vince said.

"If you don't kiss me soon, I'm going to get out of this shower and find those divorce papers," Jill threatened, turning her face up to his.

"About those divorce papers..." Vince paused to reacquaint himself with the taste of her lips.

"Burn them." Jill gasped as his hand holding the puff wandered between them. "Shred them." Jill moaned when he found just the right spot to clean.

"They weren't exactly...legal."

"Vince!"

He lifted Jill into his arms and carried her rather indelicately out of the shower.

"Vince, I need a towel. And then you're going to tell me about those papers." But Jill was clinging to him as if she never wanted to let go.

"I packed the towels yesterday."

"Tell me what you meant when you said—"

"They're not legal. It's *confuseze*." Moving with deliberate care, he laid Jill down on top of the bare mattress and covered her body gently with his. "The first page looks legit, but the rest of the pages are just filled with nonsensical legal phrases formatted to look like a legal document."

"If I had read it through—"

"You'd show up here mad as hell accusing me of being a manipulative liar." He nudged her legs apart and came to rest at home base, waiting for the signal to steal home. Although Vince wasn't stealing anything. Jill loved him. She wouldn't have given up everything for him if she didn't.

It was funny how things hadn't ended up anywhere near the way Vince had planned a few weeks ago when he rolled into Railroad Stop. He was lucky he was such a screwup.

"Oh, Vince, you're—"

"An idiot, I know. The day before I left you, I promised myself I'd come clean—no more lies. But I couldn't let you go completely. I loved you too much even if I hadn't realized it yet." Vince combed Jill's hair out of her eyes. "So I told my lawyer what to do. He had some concerns about being disbarred, but he went ahead and I'm sorry."

"If you'd let me finish a sentence." She was pouting again as she ran her fingers up his arms. "I was going to say you're brilliant, except I'm dripping wet and I don't have a towel."

Vince licked the drops from the tops of her breasts. "Let me be your towel."

"Oh. I think you missed a spot...lower." Jill speared her fingers through his hair, drawing him closer.

"Wife." Vince chuckled against her skin. He moved to fulfill her every wish and maybe a few of his own.

* * * * *

RUFUS, as Crystal Hayes had decided to call the black Lab, slept soundly on the soft seat even as she maneuvered the Softco truck in front of the Dean Grosso garage. Engines fired through the open bay doors, compressors clacked and impact tools whined as the teams tweaked their race cars in preparation for qualifying at the third race in Charlotte.

As always when she visited the garage area, Crystal experienced a vicarious thrill, watching the technicians' meticulous, last-minute preparations. As the daughter of a machinist, she understood the difference a fraction of a degree or a thousandth of an inch could make in the performance of a race car.

She muscled the driver's door shut behind her and waved hello to a couple of familiar crew members in their white-and-pale-blue jumpsuits. Then she rounded the back of the truck and rolled up the door. Inside, five boxes were marked Cargill Motors.

One of them was big and heavy, and it had slid forward a few feet, probably when she'd braked to make the narrow parking lot entrance. So she pushed up the sleeves of her canary-yellow T-shirt, then stretched forward to reach the box. A couple of catcalls came her way as her faded blue jeans tightened across her rear end. But she knew they were good-natured, and she simply ignored them.

She dragged the box toward her over the gritty metal floor.

"Let me give you a hand with that," a deep, melodious voice rumbled in her ear.

"I can manage," she responded crisply, not wanting to engage with any of the catcallers.

Here in the garage, the last thing she needed was one of the guys treating her as if she was something other than, well, one of the guys.

She'd learned long ago there was something about her that made men toss out pickup lines like parade candy. And she'd been around race crews long enough to know she needed to behave like a buddy, not a potential date.

She piled the smaller boxes on top of the large one.

"It looks heavy," said the voice.

"I'm tough," she assured him as she scooped the pile into her arms.

He didn't move away, so she turned her head to subject him to a *back off* stare. But she found herself staring into a compelling pair of green...no, brown... no, hazel eyes. She did a double take as they seemed to twinkle, multicolored, under the garage lights.

The man insistently held out his hands for the boxes. There was a dignity in his tone and little crinkles around his eyes that hinted at wisdom. There wasn't a single sign of flirtation in his expression, but Crystal was still cautious.

"You know I'm being paid to move this, right?" she asked him.

"That doesn't mean I can't be a gentleman."

Somebody whistled from a workbench. "Go, Professor Larry."

The man named Larry tossed a "Back off" over his shoulder. Then he turned to Crystal. "Sorry about that."

"Are you for real?" she asked, growing uncomfortable with the attention they were drawing. The last thing she needed was some latter-day Sir Galahad defending her honor at the track.

He quirked a dark eyebrow in a question.

"I mean," she elaborated, "you don't need to worry. I've been fending off the wolves since I was seventeen."

"Doesn't make it right," he countered, attempting to lift the boxes from her hands.

She jerked back. "You're not making it any easier."

He frowned.

"You carry this box, and they start thinking of me as a girl."

Professor Larry dipped his gaze to take in the curves of her figure. "Hate to tell you this," he said, a little twinkle coming into those multifaceted eyes.

Something about his look made her shiver inside. It was a ridiculous reaction. Guys had given her the once-over a million times. She'd learned long ago to ignore it.

"Odds are," Larry continued, a teasing drawl in his tone, "they already have."

She turned pointedly away, boxes in hand as she marched across the floor. She could feel him watching her from behind.

* * * * *

Crystal Hayes could do without her looks,
men obsessed with her looks, and guys who think
they're God's gift to the ladies.
Would Larry be the one guy who could blow all
of Crystal's preconceptions away?
Look for OVERHEATED
by Barbara Dunlop.
On sale July 29, 2008.

Silhouette®

SPECIAL EDITION

A late-night walk on the beach resulted
in Trevor Marlowe's heroic rescue of a
drowning woman. He took the amnesia
victim in and dubbed her Venus, for the
goddess who'd emerged from the sea.
It looked as if she might be his goddess of
love, too…until her former fiancé showed
up on Trevor's doorstep.

Don't miss

THE BRIDE WITH NO NAME

by *USA TODAY* bestselling author
MARIE FERRARELLA

*Available August
wherever you buy books.*

Harlequin® Historical
Historical Romantic Adventure!

From *USA TODAY*
bestselling author
Margaret Moore

A LOVER'S KISS

A Frenchwoman in London,
Juliette Bergerine is unexpectedly
thrown together in hiding with
Sir Douglas Drury. As lust and
desire give way to deeper emotions,
how will Juliette react on discovering
that her brother was murdered—
by Drury!

*Available September
wherever you buy books.*

HH29508

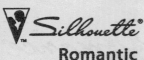

Romantic
SUSPENSE

**Sparked by Danger,
Fueled by Passion.**

Cindy Dees
Killer Affair

Seduction in the sand…and a killer on the beach.

Can-do girl Madeline Crummby is off to a remote
Fijian island to review an exclusive resort, and she hires
Tom Laruso, a burned-out bodyguard, to fly her there
in spite of an approaching hurricane. When their plane
crashes, they are trapped on an island with a serial killer
who stalks overaffectionate couples. When their false
attempts to lure out the killer turn all too real, Tom and
Madeline must risk their lives and their hearts….

**Look for the third installment
of this thrilling miniseries,
available August 2008
wherever books are sold.**

COMING NEXT MONTH

#1506 MATTHEW'S CHILDREN • C.J. Carmichael
Three Good Men
Rumor at their law firm cites Jane Prentice as the reason for Matthew Gray's divorce. The truth is, however, Jane avoids him—and not because he's a single dad. But when they're assigned to the same case, will they be able to ignore the sparks between them?

#1507 NOT ON HER OWN • Cynthia Reese
Count on a Cop
His uncle lost his best farmland to a crook, and now Brandon Wilkes is losing his heart and his pride to the crook's granddaughter...who refuses to leave the land her grandfather stole from them! How can he possibly be friends with Penelope Langston?

#1508 A PLACE CALLED HOME • Margaret Watson
The McInnes Triplets
It was murder in self-defense, and Zoe McInnes thinks she's put her past behind her. Until the brother of her late husband shows up, and Gideon Tate's own issues make him determined to seek revenge. Not even her sisters can help Zoe out of this mess. Besides, she thinks maybe Gideon is worth all the trouble he's putting her through...and more.

#1509 MORE THAN A MEMORY • Roz Denny Fox
Going Back
Seven years ago Garret Logan was devastated when his fiancée, Colleen, died in a car accident. He's tried to distract himself with work, but he hasn't been able to break free of her memory. Until the day she walks back into his pub with a new name, claiming not to remember him...

#1510 WORTH FIGHTING FOR • Molly O'Keefe
The Mitchells of Riverview Inn
Jonah Closky will do anything for his mom. That's the only reason he's at this inn to meet his estranged father and brothers. Still, there is an upside to being here: Daphne Larson. With the attraction between them, he can't think of a better way to pass the time.

#1511 SAME TIME NEXT SUMMER• Holly Jacobs
Everlasting Love
When tragedy strikes Carolyn Kendal's daughter, it's Carolyn's first love, Stephan Foster, who races to her side. A lifetime of summers spent together has taught them to follow their hearts. But after so much time apart—and the reappearance of her daughter's father—will their hearts lead them to each other?

HSRCNM0708